Gen

10667098

WITHDRAWN

NOV 7 1990

3.98

WITHDRAWN
THE PROPERTY OF
COATESVILLE PUBLIC LIBRARY

Feb 1968

BY THE AUTHOR

Dancing Horses
Blackface Stallion
The Last Summer
Grip, a Dog Story
Running Wild
The Mysterious Appearance of Agnes
Just a Dog
Russian Blue
Moshie Cat
Stallion of the Sands
Leon
The Wild Horse of Santander
The Greyhound
The Wild Heart
Horse in the Clouds

Rafa's Dog

Rafa's Dog

HELEN GRIFFITHS

Holiday House / New York

© Helen Griffiths 1983
First American publication 1983 by Holiday House, Inc.
Printed in the United States of America

Library of Congress Cataloging in Publication Data

Griffiths, Helen.
Rafa's Dog.

Summary: A Spanish child who befriends a stray dog
finds that relationship helpful when tragedy strikes
his family.
[1. Dogs—Fiction. 2. Death—Fiction. 3. Spain—
Fiction] I. Title.
PZ7.G8837Raf 1983   [Fic]   83-4384
ISBN 0-8234-0492-7

1

Mama was going to have a baby. Rafa, who was eleven years old, knew all about babies. He knew she was going to go into hospital for a few days and that the doctors there would deliver it.

His sister Conchi thought she knew all about babies, too. She was always playing with her dolls, bathing them, changing their clothes, putting powder on their plastic bottoms, and smacking them or covering them with kisses. When Rafa told her you didn't smack babies, she didn't believe him.

'If they're naughty you have to smack them,' she told him. 'How are they going to learn to be good?'

'Babies are never naughty,' Rafa said, remembering how Conchi had once been a baby. She was six years younger than him and he didn't remember as much as he pretended.

'They're always crying and messing their nappies and being sick,' said Conchi. 'Sonia's baby is, anyway.'

Sonia was her best friend. She lived in the flat upstairs and quite often they could all hear Sonia's baby sister crying and crying, night after night.

'But that's not because they're naughty. It's because they can't help it. They don't know any better,' Rafa patiently explained.

'Well, I smack my babies when they do dirty things and when they keep crying,' Conchi said with a pout, her round, dark eyes defying her brother to argue with her. She liked disagreeing with him. He was far too bossy, and he thought he knew everything.

'And why does Mama have to go to hospital to have the baby?' she wanted to know. 'Sonia's baby sister, she came from Paris. She told me. The doctor brought her all the way from Paris in his black bag.'

Rafa turned serious eyes on his sister, not certain what to say. There was an artful slant to the way she met his look, and she was a mixture of slyness and innocence. Did she really know all about babies, the same as he did? Did she half know? Was she provoking him to find out?

Papa said it was too soon to tell Conchi about babies. 'She's still only a baby herself,' he said. So when she asked awkward questions – Why was Mama getting fat? How did they know she was having a baby? Why couldn't she have it sooner? all sorts of things – Mama and Papa invented all sorts of answers which afterwards Conchi told to her friends.

'Well,' said Rafa at last thoughtfully, 'the doctor takes the baby to the hospital, you see. To make sure it's all right after being in the bag so long. And then Mama goes to collect it.'

'But why does he have to bring it from Paris? Why can't it come from Madrid, like we do? Or from Burgos, like Sonia. I asked Sonia where she came from and she said from Burgos. So why do babies come from Paris? Did I come from Paris?'

'All babies come from Paris,' Rafa explained. 'But they take them to different hospitals, wherever the mothers live. If we didn't live in Madrid, when they brought our baby they'd bring it to the hospital nearest to where we lived.'

'Mmm,' said Conchi. She was satisfied for the moment.

But Rafa was worried. He was worried because he knew a lot more than Conchi. He'd heard his parents talking two nights before, when they thought he was asleep. The bedroom door, which gave onto the living room, was open because Conchi was scared of having the door shut. He and Conchi shared a room because the flat they lived in was such a small one. And Rafa heard his parents talking.

'It'll be all right, I know it will,' Mama had said. 'It's a good hospital and everyone says Don Alfredo's a marvellous doctor.'

'But last time . . . with Conchi. You nearly died.' Papa sounded scared.

'That was last time. Six years ago. Doctors know a lot more these days. Don't worry. I trust Don Alfredo.'

'But we'll send the children to the village?'

'Yes, we'll do that. They are a bit of a strain now.'

'They'll love it there,' said Papa. 'It's the right life for a child. Not this living in the streets, swallowing petrol fumes on the way to school, and contamination on the way back.'

Papa had a thing about contamination. He was always going on about it, as if it were a person against whom he bore an eternal grudge. He blamed the government.

'They should do something. It's their fault. People who contaminate things should be locked up.'

Rafa once asked him, 'Who are they, the ones who contaminate things?'

'All these people with lorries and cars to start with,' said Papa.

'We've got a car,' said Rafa.

'Yes, but ours is only a little one. And it's old. Our sort of car came out before contamination. It's the new cars. And the lorries.'

Rafa didn't argue. Papa was right about most things, and perhaps it was true about their car.

Rafa hadn't heard any more. Perhaps he'd fallen asleep. The next day he expected Mama or Papa to start telling them about going to the village, but they hadn't said anything at all. He didn't say anything, either. Maybe it was all a dream, anyway. But he was scared. He didn't

7

know you could die having a baby. If Mama died . . .

Rafa couldn't think any further than that. Mama couldn't die. But there was a boy at school. His mother died. Not having a baby. She'd been run over, doing the shopping.

'It's the life we lead nowadays,' Papa had cried out when he heard about it, and he banged his clenched hands on the table. 'All these cars, and rushing about, and people dropping down dead with contamination . . . and no one knowing where they're going. What a life we live! Now, in the village . . .'

When he wasn't going on about contamination, Rafa's father talked about the village. His village, where he had been born and where he had grown up. It was a village in La Mancha, about a hundred and twenty miles to the south, but Rafa's father made it sound as though it was in another world.

Everything there was healthy. The people were healthy, the food was healthy, the air was healthy (no contamination *there*) the fields and houses and streets, the life people led and the way they behaved. Healthy.

When he started talking about the village, Rafa and Conchi would chant, 'Healthy, healthy, healthy,' laughing at him, making their mother laugh too, but he didn't mind.

'Well, it's true,' he'd shout at them.

And he'd tell them about the bread, hot from the ovens, that didn't go rock hard overnight; and the hams, that were the best in Spain (never mind what other people said); and the cheese . . . Well, everyone knew that the cheese from La Mancha was Number One.

'And just look at the price of it!' Mama would exclaim. She was from Madrid herself and didn't think much of the country, anyway.

'That's here, in Madrid. In the village, they almost give it away,' Papa boasted.

8

As for the wine! Papa would bunch his fingers together and kiss the tips, with an ecstatic, faraway look in his eyes.

'Healthy!' they'd all shout, faces shining with laughter.

Rafa had been to the village once, when he was about six, but he couldn't remember much about it. He knew his uncle had a donkey called Ana, and he remembered riding on its rump. And it galloped off down the street with him and he fell off and split his head open on the stones. He still had the scar, and always would have.

Once he said to Papa, 'Well, I don't think the village is very healthy, not for me, anyway. I almost got killed there.'

And Papa exclaimed, 'Bah! That's nothing. When I was a boy in the village, all the boys used to gang up and have battles. We used to throw stones at each other, try and pinch each other's territory. Look!'

He took hold of Rafa's hand and made him push his fingers through the hair on the left side of his head. There was a dent there, quite a deep one.

'Knocked me out for three days, that did. Would've killed a city boy.'

Conchi had to feel it next. She drew back with a shudder, her lip curled up with disgust. She didn't like anything that was creepy or ugly, or dirty, or strange. She still screamed at cockroaches and in summertime said to Mama every night, 'Don't forget to put the powder down.'

Mama put powder on the floor across the bedroom door so the cockroaches couldn't get into their bedroom. They stopped to eat the powder, and then they died. They turned over on their backs and their legs wriggled about in agony, and Mama had to make sure she'd swept them all away before Conchi got up, otherwise she'd scream and scream.

Rafa always felt sorry for them. They couldn't help being cockroaches, and they didn't hurt you, or bite you or anything. They lived in the cracks because it was an old, old

9

house, and they came out to eat up any dirt they could find. So, really, cockroaches were doing you a favour, Rafa thought.

But Mama hated them, too. Mama was always cleaning, and when the cockroaches appeared she took it as a personal insult. Her floor tiles were spotless. She washed and oiled them every day, and swept up the kitchen every night before going to bed, so they should go somewhere else to do their scavenging – not act as if they expected a good feast in her house every night.

'I'll give them a feast,' she threatened.

And so she did. She bought boxes of poisoned powder at the hardware store and they ate it up and died. And those that didn't die must have told their friends there was this lovely powder to eat, because what else would they come for, except for that?

Did cockroaches know about dying? Or did it just happen to them? It just happened to the boy at school's mother. She was crossing the road and . . .

Rafa shut his eyes suddenly. It made him breathless just to think such things.

He was sitting on the little kitchen balcony, five storeys above the street. The green wooden blind hung over the iron railing, keeping the sun off his head, making a striped pattern on his bare legs. You could see over all the rooftops from this balcony, slopes of red tiles, broken by attic windows slipping out of shape and a forest of television aerials, all baking and shimmering beneath the deep blue sky.

It was Rafa's favourite place, the place where he came to think, to dream, to be alone. Conchi was sitting on the floor, surrounded by dolls, talking and muttering to them. She was only just out of arm's reach but she could have been a million miles away. He looked over the roofs and up at the sky, and he was alone in the world.

Even in wintertime he sat there, hunched up in a jacket, with the shutters pulled to, making it even more private. And Mama would shout, 'Rafa, it's too cold out there. Come in,' but he'd pretend not to hear her, so she left him.

Perhaps she knew that in this tall, narrow house, crowded with people, surrounded by other tall, narrow houses almost touching each other across the narrowest of grey streets, where the sun hardly reached, that he had found a place that was his alone. He shared it with the small bits of washing and the pots of dangling geraniums that died every winter but came back to life every spring, and as he got taller the balcony got smaller. Even Conchi knew it was Rafa's balcony. She played on the staircase landing with her friends.

Rafa thought, 'If they're going to send us to the village, they'll have to tell us beforehand. And if they don't tell us, that means I did dream it. And if I dreamt it, then it's not true. Mama's not going to die. Not ever.'

2

Papa waited until it was his day off to tell them. He was a waiter at a hotel in the city centre, so he nearly always worked on Sundays, when other fathers stayed at home. His day off was Thursday, which was all right when they were on holiday, but not much fun when they were at school.

In holiday time on Papa's day off Mama would put a picnic lunch in her shopping bag; Conchi would pack a little straw basket with her zinc pots and pans and a doll or two; Rafa would get his black and white football from under his bed; Papa would put the old magazines he got from work under his arm, and they would get into Papa's little secondhand Seat and set out for a day in the country.

There was never much traffic on the motorway on a Thursday and Papa really enjoyed himself, driving along with the windows down, breathing in the Castilian air, 'Getting away from the contamination,' he would constantly remind them. They'd shout jokes and riddles at each other and sometimes sing. Conchi knew lots of songs from nursery school.

They'd find a place where there was shade, trees and a river, and they'd play football – Papa and Rafa – while Mama put out the food and chased big black ants off the tablecloth she'd set out on the sandy ground. Conchi did the same sort of thing with her dolls.

After eating, Papa always went to sleep for an hour or so, snoring with his mouth open. Mama would find somewhere to clean the plates, while Conchi fell asleep on the back seat of the car. Rafa would wander around, kicking up the dust with his sandals, filling up ant holes which were as round as pencils, and wishing they were back in the city, which wasn't half so boring as being on a patch of sun-baked ground miles away from nowhere.

They did this every Thursday in the summertime and Papa always said that one day, when he got a better job, or more money, they'd have a proper holiday somewhere – all of them together. Maybe at the seaside.

'Like the foreigners,' said Papa. 'We'll stay in a hotel and Mama won't have to wash any dishes or make any beds or do any cooking.'

'That'd be a dream!' she always exclaimed.

They always said the same sort of things. Rafa wondered if they noticed. They didn't seem to. Grown ups were always repeating themselves.

But this particular Thursday, while they were sitting round the flowery tablecloth, each with half a loaf into which a cold, breadcrumbed steak was stuffed, Papa suddenly exclaimed, 'Well, children, it'll be the real country life for you soon. You'll like that, won't you?'

Rafa felt himself going stiff with fear. Conchi just stared, waiting for him to explain.

'It's a holiday,' he said. 'In the village. While Mama has the baby. When you come back, there'll be a new brother or sister waiting for you. Won't that be lovely?'

'Why've we got to go to the village?' said Rafa.

'Because new babies make a lot of work at first,' Mama answered him, 'and I'll be tired and won't want to be washing and cooking. Papa can eat at the hotel, but you two . . .'

'I can help with the baby,' cried Conchi. 'I know all about babies. Sonia's Mama lets me watch. But I don't want to change its nappies. Ugh! That's horrible. Will our baby be dirty, Mama? I don't like dirty babies. Will ours be clean?'

'Not at first. Later . . .'

'That's why,' broke in Papa, 'we're sending you to the village. You'll have a lovely time with the family.'

'We hardly know them,' said Rafa coldly.

'But you'll like them. They're very friendly. Everyone's friendly in the village.'

'Can I take my dolls?' asked Conchi.

'Of course you can, sweetheart!' Papa exclaimed happily, glad he'd got over one hurdle so easily.

'I want to stay with Mama,' said Rafa. 'I can do the shopping. I'll eat bread and cheese. She won't need to cook.'

'Don't be such a donkey,' was Mama's cross reply. She always called him a donkey when he was stubborn. Usually it made him angry. But today . . . He stared hard at her. He couldn't understand.

Surely, if . . . Wasn't she scared? Didn't she know he wanted to be with her, had to stay with her? How could they send him to that village, where he wouldn't know what was happening, whether Mama was all right?

'Why do you look at me like that?' she exclaimed.

His face was pale, and stiff like a stone, his eyes dark circles of fear. He looked down at the tablecloth, seeing its green and yellow flowers blur into muddled shapes. Then he threw down his bread and rushed off among the trees.

'Rafa!'

He heard her call his name, but he didn't stop, stumbling on with mind torn and muddled. Mama was going to die and they didn't want him there. They were sending him away. Conchi, too. They'd never see Mama again.

Perhaps they'd be in that horribly healthy village for ever, with horribly healthy bumpkin louts who threw stones at each other for fun.

'Rafa! Rafa!' This time it was Papa.

14

He came running after him and caught up with him, grabbing his arm.

'What's the matter with you?' he said, sounding more bewildered than cross.

'I heard you and Mama talking the other night . . . About when Conchi was born.' He kept his head down as he painfully mumbled out the words, not wanting to see the truth in his father's face.

'But that was a long time ago, Rafa. Things are different now.'

'That's what Mama said. And you didn't believe her. You think . . .'

He shot an anguished look at his father, pleading. He didn't want it to be true. But he couldn't really tell what Papa was thinking even when he replied, 'I don't think anything of the sort.'

'You did the other night. I heard you. Conchi was asleep. But I heard you. You were scared.'

'No, no,' Papa protested. 'You got it wrong. You were half asleep.'

He put his hands on Rafa's shoulders and squeezed. He stared at him and there was a look of love in his eyes.

'I wouldn't tell you a lie, son.'

'You tell Conchi lies.'

'Me? Never! When?'

'About the baby. She asks you about it and you tell her lies.'

Papa looked relieved.

'That's different,' he laughed. 'She's only little. She doesn't understand.'

'She would if you told her.'

'Not yet. Not yet.'

'Maybe you think I don't understand, about Mama.'

Papa put an arm round Rafa's shoulders and started to

15

walk with him. They walked under the trees, where the sun spread dappled patterns and a column of black ants poured in an organized stream round a rock, along a crack in the ground, and across the sand towards a recently discarded sardine tin. The air was noisy with crickets.

Rafa knew Papa was trying to think of the right words to say.

'Look,' he began at last. 'Your mother's not very strong. It's her heart. When she was about your age she had a fever. It affected her heart. And having a baby is hard work. But Don Alfredo – that's the doctor – he's a specialist. Knows all about hearts. He's going to be there, and everything's going to be all right.'

'Do you promise, Papa?'

Never had Rafa stared so hard into his father's eyes before. They were blue, almost like the sky. Mama was always saying, 'Why doesn't Conchi have her father's eyes? Oh, I do like blue eyes, and they're so pretty in a girl!' Mama's eyes were brown, like his and Conchi's. Papa said that nearly everyone in his village had blue eyes.

Papa rubbed his hand through Rafa's hair.

'I love your mother very much,' he said. 'No one's going to take her away from me. Or from you!' he shouted. 'She's the best mother in the world.' He grinned. 'Come on. Let's go back. We don't want to worry her. Don't let her know what you heard. She'll be upset. Just tell her it's because you don't want to go to the village.'

'I don't. Let me stay at home, Papa. Just send Conchi. She makes all the work. Not me. I'll help.'

He shook his head.

'Mama will rest much better if there's no one to have things to do for. She wouldn't stay in bed if she's got to iron your shirt or get your dinner. You know what she's like. You be a good boy and go to the village. And as soon as Don Alfredo says it's all right, you can come home again. I promise.'

3

They went to the village on Papa's next day off. They were going to go by car but the little blue Seat had something wrong with the radiator so they had to go by coach. Mama didn't go with them. She wanted to but she was feeling too tired.

It was so hot. For several days the Sahara wind had been blowing across the whole country and people were almost gasping for breath. Rafa always thought the wind was cheating when it blew so hot. Winds were supposed to be fresh, cool, but this one was like hot air coming from an oven, and there was nowhere you could turn to escape it.

At night they sat round the table with an electric fan humming away, whizzing out cold air, but that was only all right as long as you stayed right next to it. Conchi managed to sleep. 'She still sleeps like a baby,' said Mama, wistfully, but everyone else just lay in the dark, too exhausted to move, sighing and panting.

'One day we're going to have air conditioning,' said Papa. But air conditioning cost a lot of money and, besides, the electric wiring in the house was out of date.

The coach station was only a ten-minute walk from their house so Mama came to see them off. Conchi had a plastic bag with dolls poking out and her pots and pans banging against her leg. Rafa helped Papa with a suitcase.

There were seat numbers on the tickets but people still argued about where to sit. Nobody wanted to sit on the sunny side, even with the blinds down, so it was just as well they had numbers. Otherwise, some of them might have ended up having a fight. The driver came and restored order, shouting at everybody, and then they were off – waving to Mama, who wouldn't go until they were out of sight, even though Papa kept telling her not to stand around.

The coach had air conditioning. There were buttons above your head that you could twist to make the air from outside come in the way you wanted it to. The trouble was the air was hot, so it wasn't much good, but both Rafa and Conchi enjoyed themselves playing with the buttons.

Conchi was sitting by the window with Papa, and Rafa was on the seat behind. There was an old woman next to him who looked as though she'd never heard of progress – as if she'd come straight from her village, almost from the previous century. She was dressed in black, from the shawl that covered her head to the stockings and cloth shoes on her twisted feet. It was such an old black, with stains on it, that Rafa tried to pretend she wasn't there.

She kept talking to him and he had to answer, to be polite, but he could hardly understand her accent and didn't even know if she could hear him. She kept putting her hand to her ear and saying, 'What? What?' so he had to shout. When he looked out of the window, pretending not to hear, she clawed at his arm to get his attention. Conchi made faces at him over the back of her seat and laughed. She thought it was funny.

The old woman fell asleep and Rafa was left to his thoughts. At first looking out of the window was interesting, but soon it got very boring because the scenery was all the same. Mile after mile of scorched flat landscape, with the odd, lonely house here and there, a donkey dozing under a tree with flopping ears; browns, yellows, yellows, browns, until his eyes ached with looking.

He wondered what Mama was doing. Had she gone

home to rest like Papa had told her? She was very fat now. The baby was going to be born in just a couple of weeks. She was making little clothes for it, getting things ready, and Papa had bought a cot (because they didn't have Conchi's any more). It was chromium plated and very shiny, and it had a plastic mattress with little bears and rabbits on it.

He wondered what the people in the village would be like. He vaguely knew them by name and he remembered his aunt and uncle a little because from time to time they had come to Madrid on business.

Papa said Aunt Meri's real name was Emerenciana, but no one ever called her that. It was too much of a mouthful. She was Papa's sister and she was older than him. She had a son who was doing his military service at an airforce base in the north, and a daughter who was studying to be a teacher. She was on holiday in Ireland just then, learning English, so neither of them were at home.

Uncle Fat was her husband. Rafa and Conchi always laughed about Uncle Fat. Fancy having a name like that! It wasn't his real name, of course, and the silliest thing about it was that he wasn't fat at all. He was no fatter than Papa, lean and muscled from all the work he did in the fields.

'What's his real name?' Conchi had asked, but Papa couldn't remember. He only knew that his brother-in-law had been the fattest boy in the school, and the fattest young man in the village. By the time he started to get thin no one called him anything but Fat. Not even his wife. It was his name now. For ever. That's what village people were like.

Rafa was still dreading this holiday in the village, even though he wasn't scared about Mama any more. He had a city boy's scorn for country people. If a new boy came to school from a village, everyone called him a bumpkin. When Rafa told his friend, Antonio, that he was going to the village, Antonio had laughed at him and said, 'You'll be a real bumpkin by the time you come back.'

He started talking with a bumpkin voice, and crossing his eyes, to make fun of Rafa. 'That'll be you,' he laughed. 'Smelling like a donkey, and braying like one.'

They had a very satisfactory fight. Rafa twisted Antonio's arm till he promised not to insult him any more, and he even promised to write a letter and tell Rafa what was going on in Madrid while he was away. He wouldn't write. Rafa hadn't given him an address.

The miles and the hours went by and Rafa dozed, seeing yellow deserts and scrubby hills even in his dreams. When he woke up they were half way there and the coach had stopped so people could stretch their legs, have a drink and go to the toilet.

He and Conchi had some orange juice and Conchi suddenly said, 'Can we go home now? I'm fed up. I want to go home.'

'But we haven't got to the village yet,' Papa told her.

'Don't want to go to the village. I want to go home.'

Papa tried to explain again. Rafa helped him but Conchi was tired and hot and cross. She just kept on wailing, 'I want to go home. I want to be with Mama,' until Papa bought her a little doll to shut her up. He looked pretty desperate by then. Rafa could have whacked her one himself. She was a spoilt little brat.

Uncle Fat met them at the coach station in Ciudad Real. He had a really big car, not a bit like Papa's, and it had almost new number plates. He picked Conchi up in his brown, sinewy arms and hugged her so tight that she squealed, and to Rafa he said, 'How are you, son?' pinching his cheek so hard that Rafa had to blink away tears of agony.

It was about seven o'clock and they were all hungry and tired. Uncle Fat put the cases in the boot and shot them out of the city streets as if he was the only driver on the road. People shouted at him and he shouted back. Once they were on the road to the village, he put his foot down on the accelerator and zoomed over bumps and holes as if he could afford a new car every year.

He kept saying, 'This is marvellous. Marvellous. Who'd have thought it, you kids coming to stay? You'll have a wonderful time. Marvellous. You'll see. Your aunt can hardly wait. Everything's been ready for a week.'

And then to Papa, 'And you, Rafa? How's city life, then? Bet you wish you'd never left us. I'll give you a job if you want to come back.'

Papa didn't need any more urging. He started on about contamination, and rushing around, and not being able to earn a decent living, and how the only people with any sense were those who stayed in the villages.

'Of course, man. It's a good life when it rains in winter, and the sheep don't die, and the grapes don't get the blight. Didn't rain at all last winter.'

'Did the sheep die?' asked Conchi curiously, and Rafa rushed mischievously on, 'Did the grapes get the blight?'

Uncle Fat grinned and flung back at them, 'I can see what you two are. A pair of clever dicks. Ay, mother!' he sighed, with a shake of his head.

And, in spite of the cheek that still stung, Rafa decided that he liked him.

4

Rafa had looked for Papa's village on the map of Spain in his school atlas, but he couldn't find it. Papa said it was too small to put on an ordinary map, and not important enough to be mentioned in the history books. Nobody famous had been born there, no important battles had taken place. 'Not even Don Quixote passed through!' he exclaimed with a laugh.

La Mancha was the land of Don Quixote, the famous, half-mad gentleman who thought he was a knight of old and went round righting wrongs and helping damsels in distress. Rafa had read the book at school, because everybody had to read it, and now he expected to see windmills, like the one Don Quixote had fought with when he thought it was a giant.

But there weren't any windmills. Just fields of stubble where the grain had been harvested, and fields of vines with grapes too sour to be eaten. La Mancha had been an exciting world for Don Quixote, with circus people whose lion he killed; convicts on a chain gang he'd let free; bandits who robbed and beat him; and princesses who were no more than kitchen maids. But so far Rafa had found no one and nothing at all worth a second glance.

He had gone out like Don Quixote, seeking adventure, leaving Conchi at his aunt's house, playing dolls with some girls from across the street. Aunt Meri had said it was much too hot to go out, that he ought to wait till evening, but she was a fusspot – large and kindly, but still a fusspot – and he soon tired of staying indoors.

He wandered off down the street with his football for company, dribbling it along the lanes and losing it for a minute under a mule cart that came lumbering round a corner. All the time he felt very conscious of being a stranger – 'the boy from Madrid' as everyone already called him – so he concentrated on the football, trying to make it look as though he hadn't a care in the world.

Soon he'd come to the end of the village. There was the track that led to the main road, and all that was ahead of him were sun-scorched fields, promising . . . what?

Aunt Meri had been right about the sun. It was far too hot to be out in, but Rafa didn't want to go back. Overlooking the village, seemingly not very far away, he had spied the ruins of a Moorish castle, sinking into the hilltop on which it had been built ten centuries before. If he cut across the fields, surely it wouldn't take him long to get there?

He picked up the football, tucked it under his arm, and strode along purposefully. The stubble crackled under his feet and began digging through the gaps in his sandals, right through his socks, scratching his feet. It was far more tiring than striding along the city pavements. There were furrows and dips, stones and thistles, and there was no escape from the heat which weighed relentlessly on his shoulders.

Before he'd gone very far, Rafa decided to turn back. He'd try again in the evening. Perhaps he could go with Uncle Fat. Turning round, he saw not far off a little house sheltered behind a row of tall, thick canes, and he decided to make for that. Perhaps someone there would give him a drink of water. When he got closer he saw that the house was no more than a ruin. Still, he could stop there for a while, out of the sun, and get the bits of stalk and dust out of his sandals.

There was no door, and no glass in the window frame,

and there was just one little room, with a broken bedstead underneath the soundest part of the roof, which was half fallen in. On the bed were the remains of a striped mattress, once filled with straw. It was full of holes and Rafa shuddered, wondering if the holes might have been made by rats and, worse still, if rats might still be living in it.

But he just had to sit down for a while! He picked up a broken tile and threw it at the mattress. Nothing stirred. Perhaps it was all right.

Gratefully, he went over to the only bit of shade and sat down, putting the football, which had stuck to his arm and made a damp patch on his shirt, between his feet. He leaned against the adobe wall and shut his eyes. They were feeling sore from the glare of the sun. How he wished he had a pair of sunglasses! Ah, but it was cooler here.

This was where Moro found him.

Moro was a dog who belonged to no one. He wasn't very big. There was a hint of hunting dog in his rounded, droopy ears and long, thin tail, and the bit of white speckling on his front. But it was only a hint. His was a hotch-potch of mongrel blood that owed nothing to human intervention.

Nobody knew where or when he had been born but, as Rafa was later to discover, everyone knew he had come to the village with a man whose ancestry and history were as clouded as his own. This man was a traveller of some sort who, at one time or another, must have been kind to Moro – perhaps had thrown him a few crusts, or allowed him to share the comfort of a wayside fire. The man never said, and Moro certainly couldn't, and nobody cared anyway.

The two of them hung out in the ruined building, and the man called at every house asking people if they wanted their woollen mattresses cleaned and tossed. He offered to do it cheaper than the usual mattress man so some of the neighbours accepted, even if they didn't trust him very much and put a child to watch and make sure he didn't stick any of the valuable wool in his sack.

Moro would hang about somewhere near, keeping an eye on him, too, and if the man was silent and mysterious and slow-moving, Moro was just the opposite. He couldn't keep still for more than a minute. He got into all the houses, poked his black nose into everything, knocked over water pitchers and milk jugs, stole anything edible that might be around, and braved the women's shrieks and broom handles as they chased him out.

There was never a dog like Moro for getting into mischief and yet managing to evade sticks and stones. Threats had no effect on him. He shrugged them off with a glint of delight in his dark eyes, and having escaped his pursuers and feeling safe, would then turn round and bark at them – not with any malice, but as if to say, 'That was fun, wasn't it?'

It was no good talking to the mattress man. He just shrugged his shoulders and pretended to know nothing of Moro's carryings on. Moro had no collar or licence. You could be sure he'd never been vaccinated against rabies in all his life. He was full of fleas and ticks and when he wasn't getting into trouble, or sleeping off his adventures, he'd be scratching all day long.

The man didn't actually say so, but he gave the impression that Moro no more belonged to him than did the sun in the sky. Moro was a free agent. He could come or go or do as he liked, and if someone caught him, and in a fury beat him to death, that was Moro's problem, not his. It wasn't his fault that Moro tagged along behind him.

Moro was like the wind, blowing where it chose, or moved by some mysterious power. Moved by the devil, everyone thought, and they were glad when they knew the stranger had tossed and refilled all the mattresses people had given to him and would be moving on. Because then

25

Moro would go, too, and life in the village would go back to normal.

Nobody knew quite when the man moved on. When he wasn't squatting in the street, sewing up mattresses, or lying in the shade, asleep against a wall, Moro curled up beside him, he went back to the ruined house and his life was a mystery to them. All they discovered one day was that he'd gone and Moro hadn't. Whether this was because Moro had been off on some business of his own when the man set out on the road again, no one knew or cared, but everyone was angry.

They did their best to persuade Moro to move on, too. He was hunted down by bands of children. They harried him through just about every hour of daylight and darkness, urged on by the adults who had tired of chasing that elusive black spirit themselves.

When they caught him, as they did sometimes, they'd pull his tail and twist his ears, kick and beat him, but Moro was as slippery as a piece of wet soap and no one could hold onto him for long. He'd shoot off between their legs or outstretched hands, yelping and whimpering, but never once did he try to defend himself, except by flight.

If he knew his teeth could hurt, perhaps he also knew that his enemies were children, and on the odd occasion when a child did get a bruise or a scratch from him it would be quite accidental on Moro's part – sheer desperation, perhaps.

And yet Moro knew that it wasn't a game to them. He knew, because as soon as he saw them coming, with their sticks or stones or catapults, or just with the menace in their shouts, he'd be up and away, like a hare in the fields at the first sound of the hunters.

He'd make for the fields. There they could never catch him. They'd throw stones after him, and cruel promises. Some of them were cunning enough to call him sweetly, and offer him something to eat, but Moro took no chances when he knew their blood was up.

However, he always came back, almost as if he'd forgotten – or forgiven – their cruelty. He was always giving them another chance and, as time went by and Moro wouldn't be finished off or driven away, a kind of truce was forged between the little black dog and the village children.

Mostly now they left him alone. From time to time they'd go for him, when there was nothing better to do, or when Moro just happened to be sleeping peacefully in a corner where he could be easily trapped, an irresistible target. But there was an understanding between them. Now and again the children would throw him bits of bread they didn't want, or their chocolate papers, to tease him.

There were scars and lumps on Moro's body but seemingly none inside him, because he still went about the village as though it belonged to him. And he still sneaked into the houses and stole what he could, and chased the cats and scattered the chickens, and barked at mules, and danced around with waving tail and sparkling eyes, completely uncowed by all that had been done to him.

Perhaps it was just because he was free.

The one place that belonged to him – at least, to his canine understanding of things – was the ruined house where nobody came. This was where he hid out when his sufferings were too many, or when he just wanted a bit of peace. Nobody knew that Moro still went there. He was as cautious as a wild animal about his hiding place.

Was he waiting for the traveller to come back? Did he have good memories of the fire on the hearthstone? Did he just like having his own mattress to sleep on? These were things that probably even Moro didn't know the answer to.

But now Rafa was there, and Moro's only secret was discovered.

5

There were dogs in Madrid, though not many in Rafa's part of the city, which was very old and overcrowded, and not at all suitable for any kind of pet but canary birds, whose cages hung from walls and balconies among flowers and roller blinds. There was an old lady who had three dogs, fat, hairy mongrels that toddled all over the pavement, leaving their messes for people to tread in. Everybody disliked this old woman – or, at least, her dogs – and the shopkeepers would mutter under their breath and promise to poison them one day.

Papa always said he felt sorry for city dogs. It was bad enough for humans to have to breathe in the fog of petrol fumes, and therefore it was much worse for dogs because they had sensitive noses and were closer to all the exhaust pipes that churned out the fumes.

Papa knew about dogs because, when he'd lived in the village, he'd had a little dog of his own. It was called Perla, and was white like a pearl, and he used to sneak it into bed with him when his mother wasn't looking. But Perla disappeared one day and he never found her. Papa's father had had a hunting dog, a sort of greyhound, that chased hares across the cornfields; and the shepherds had dogs, too.

But Mama didn't like dogs. She didn't like any kind of animal. Once Conchi had brought home a kitten which the grocer was going to drown. But Mama had made her take it back, for once not heeding Conchi's tears. Rafa had wanted to keep the kitten, too, it was so small and pretty, but Mama said cats had fleas, and they scratched you and made holes in the furniture and were smelly.

Mama was afraid of dogs. When Rafa was little he used to want to stroke dogs if he saw them in the street, and Mama would cry out and snatch him away. 'Don't touch him. He'll eat you!' she'd say, and at first he believed her and was scared.

When he got older he knew dogs didn't eat you, but Conchi still thought they could. She still thought they were as bad as wolves in fairy tales, that they'd eat you as soon as look at you – even the waddly fat dogs of the neighbourhood that hardly came up to her knee.

She pretended not to be scared, but Rafa knew she was. She'd say, 'Bad dog, go away,' if one only so much as looked at her, and she'd tell Rafa to chase it off if it wouldn't go away.

Mama didn't even have a canary. She said they made a lot of work, throwing seed all over the place. Once they'd had one, when Rafa was little, and Mama forgot to bring it in from the sun one day and Rafa found it dead in the cage. After that, Mama gave the cage away and said she didn't want any more pets. They made work and cost money, and it wasn't healthy to have an animal in a flat that was almost too small for them.

So when Rafa saw Moro looking at him, one paw lifted in surprise and fear, he didn't know what to do. Then, he didn't know anything about Moro, and his first thought was that perhaps this little house belonged to Moro's owner and that the black dog had come to chase him out. But then he realized that Moro was as undecided as he was. They stared at each other, trying to figure one another out.

Moro had never found a boy in his house before. Perhaps he even knew that Rafa was a stranger. Quite possibly, by now Moro knew every boy in the village – which ones were most likely to persecute him, which had kinder hearts. It took a little while for this new situation to settle into his animal brain.

But Moro wasn't a coward and it was the very inquisitiveness of his nature that got him into so many scrapes. He couldn't just turn tail and run off without first investigating. But he was tense, prepared for anything, especially the worst. So he went on standing in the doorway, the sun gleaming on his dusty coat, one paw still half suspended, ready for flight.

And Rafa saw something in Moro that prevented him from following his first instinct, which was to shout and wave and frighten him off. There was a chunk of tile within reach, just in case the dog turned nasty, but this was only a very vague comfort at the back of Rafa's mind. Really, he was just as curious as Moro himself.

They went on staring at each other and Moro put his paw on the ground and licked his nose, cocking his head slightly to one side. He already knew that Rafa was harmless, though he too had seen the broken tile and had judged to exactness the split second he needed to dodge it. There was a friendly glow in his eyes that spread to his tail and made it start wagging. His mouth fell open and his tongue lolled out. It was really too hot to keep it in, now that danger was past.

Rafa's face split into a grin, as wide as the dog's. This was Moro's best defence, if only he was given a chance to use it, and Rafa, the city boy, fell for it straight away. If you didn't know Moro – his thieving, his clumsiness, his cheek and determination – your heart just had to melt at the instant adoration that poured from Moro's brown eyes.

Rafa made clicking noises and stretched out his hand.

For a minute Moro just looked at him, tail still wagging,

30

eyes adoring, but too accustomed to treachery to respond straight away.

'Here dog. Come here,' said Rafa.

His voice was a bit too demanding for Moro's liking. His tail wagged faster, somewhat apologetically, then he jumped on the bed – his bed now that the man who had last slept in it had gone. In nervous excitement he half hung his head over the edge of the tatty mattress, stuck his rump in the air, tail beating time above it, and looked at Rafa.

His body squirmed and jumped with excitement which suddenly burst out of him in a chorus of yaps. In his way, he was saying, 'Come here,' to Rafa. He was too scared to cross the narrow dividing line between them.

Rafa stood up, hesitating. All Mama's warnings about dogs were in his mind – fleas, diseases, bites . . . And then, before he knew it, he was beside the bed, and Moro was chasing about over the mattress like a wild thing, running in circles, yapping, yelping, clowning so madly that Rafa couldn't help laughing just to see him.

Moro jumped up in the air and planted a great, slobbering lick across Rafa's lips and then, frightened by his own daring, dashed to the far corner of the bed and crouched against the wall, dark eyes gleaming, scared, hoping, expecting . . .

Rafa sat on the bed and laughed, making Moro flatten his ears for a moment until he realized that the boy wasn't mocking him, that there was joy in his voice, not scorn. Then he crept forward until he was close enough to lay his head across Rafa's knees – body ready to recoil in an instant, trembling with longing and fear. Now his ears were flat against his head, and the look in his blue-brown eyes was one of supplication. White-ringed, they looked up into Rafa's face, and Rafa's hand came down on the scarred, dusty head in an instinctive caress.

31

Two, three times the hand stroked gently across the hard skull. Moro's tongue licked out nervously over his nose and then his head crept up towards Rafa's. Next minute the tongue was licking Rafa's neck, his ear, his cheek, and Rafa was falling backwards across the mattress under this onslaught of nervous adoration, still laughing with delight as Moro clambered all over him, whimpering, licking, wagging.

'Hey, hey!' he protested, pushing the dog away, but only because he thought he ought, not because he wanted to. And Moro knew what was going on in the boy's heart, and he threw himself on him with renewed joy, all caution abandoned as he poured out on Rafa all the love that was in him and which no one had been able to quench.

Moro followed Rafa back to the village, dancing along beside him, jumping up at his hands and legs, or rushing ahead. He barked at shadows to show Rafa what a perfect guard dog he would be, if that was what Rafa wanted. Smartly recovering from the fright of finding a bird squatting in the stubble, he chased after it with flat-eared intensity, dancing back to Rafa once it had taken to the air as if to say, 'Look, I'm a hunting dog, too.'

And Rafa forgot the sun and the stones, unable to take his eyes off this lively, comical dog that wasn't a bit like anything he expected – those fat, dirty things in Madrid, or the wolfish, ravening creatures his mother's words and his sister's fears conjured in his imagination.

He wondered who the dog belonged to, with a slight pain in his heart already that the friendship that had sprung up between them would be as brief as it was sudden. When they got to the village someone would suddenly say, 'Hey, that's my dog. What are you doing with him?' (or something like that). Or the dog itself would run off to his own home, forgetting all about him.

But when they got to the village, Moro didn't run off and

no one said anything, at least, not about the dog. They called out to Rafa, 'How's it going then? Enjoying yourself?' – things like that – and Rafa replied politely, hardly daring to take his eyes off Moro, expecting him to run off at any moment.

But Moro had no intention of running off. Rafa was his, or he was Rafa's – it didn't matter which and he didn't work it out like that anyway. He just knew that Rafa's hands were gentle and that there was no malice in him. And, for a start anyway, that was enough for Moro.

A couple of dolls were lying in the passage under the house, next to a half empty plastic washing bowl, when Rafa got back with Moro, but Conchi and the other girls had disappeared. Moro immediately thrust his head into the bowl and began desperately lapping at the water, swallowing soap bubbles and all, while Rafa stood and watched, and wondered if his new-found friend might be as hungry as he was thirsty.

'Are you hungry, dog?' he asked, and Moro looked up sharply, as if understanding the question. His tail wagged and his eyes gleamed, then he dunked his nose back in the bowl and went on lapping.

It was just as well Conchi wasn't around, Rafa decided. She'd be screaming her head off by now. And where was Aunt Meri? Would she give him something for the black dog to eat?

He went through to the patio, which was full of tall plants. Aunt Meri said at one time the patio used to be a corral for the sheep, but Uncle Fat had changed it. He had put in a sink, with running water, where Aunt Meri did the washing, and under the sink, where it was cool, there was a big jug of milk covered by a dish. Did dogs like milk, Rafa wondered?

They certainly did because before he knew it Moro, who had followed him into the patio and watched him lift the dish, was sticking his nose into the jug, lapping eagerly.

33

'Hey, get out of it!' cried Rafa, and Moro sprang away, ears flat, body suddenly hunched and trembling.

Rafa was contrite. He hadn't meant to scare him. Poor little dog. He really must be hungry.

'Wait here,' he told him. 'I'll see what I can find.'

If he'd been at home, Rafa would have known exactly where to look for things, but Aunt Meri's house was still strange to him. He went into the kitchen and pulled open cupboards, and in a minute Moro was there beside him, sticking his head into everything, almost getting it shut in when Rafa wanted to close the doors again.

Aunt Meri wasn't there, which was just as well, Rafa decided, feeling she wouldn't be too pleased about the dog. At least, she wouldn't if she was anything like Mama. But village people were different. Hadn't Papa taken his own dog to bed? So it must have been allowed in the house. And if Papa had kept a dog, then Aunt Meri must be used to dogs, too.

Eventually he found a plastic bag full of buns and cakes. He knew they were good because he and Conchi had had some for breakfast, with a bowl of coffee. He broke off a piece of cake and offered it to the dog.

Moro zamped it in a second. 'Gosh, you are hungry!' exclaimed Rafa, a big grin on his face as he gave him the next bit, and the next. The cake was gone.

The bag was full so he took out another, then another, and another, and Moro sat on the red-tiled floor and looked at him, begging with his eyes, his ears, his whole body until Rafa – somewhat reluctantly – offered him a fifth.

He refused to give him any more after that, so Moro ran round in circles snuffling up the crumbs, leaving little wet patches on the tiles. Then Rafa remembered the milk, found a basin and filled it almost to the brim. Moro drank the lot without stopping and he licked and licked the basin as if to show just how much he liked it.

'You can't still be hungry!' cried Rafa. It was true that the dog was a bit on the thin side – there was just the shadow of his ribs under the shiny, dusty skin – but five cakes and a basin full of milk . . .

Just then Aunt Meri arrived.

'Rafa!' she exclaimed with horror. 'What's that dog doing in my house?'

Of a sudden, kind Aunt Meri turned into a fury. A broom appeared in her hands with which she ferociously intended to sweep Moro out of her kitchen. The dog ran in circles round Rafa. He longed to escape but, with one eye on Rafa, and one on the broom, and both now and again on his whirlwind attacker, he just couldn't find the door.

'Don't hit him, don't hit him!' cried Rafa. 'I'll take him out.'

'Not hit him! I'll murder him if I find him in my kitchen again. Go on. Shoo. Get out. Rogue. Thief. Vagabond.'

With every insult she thrust the broom at poor Moro, getting it tangled in Rafa's legs as he desperately tried to stop her. In the confusion, Moro found an escape route and disappeared. Within seconds only Rafa and Aunt Meri were left in the kitchen, the empty basin lying broken between them (the broom had landed right on it in one of Aunt Meri's attacks).

They hurried to the patio, with different intentions, and then to the passage, but Moro had gone. Rafa went as far as the street, screwing up his eyes against the sun's glare. His heart was beating fast, and he was holding back tears of anger as he looked up and down the long lane of white-walled houses.

There wasn't even a whisper of the little black dog. How could he vanish so quickly? Would he ever come back again?

6

By lunchtime Uncle Fat had come back from the city. He had gone there early in the morning with Papa, who had caught the first coach to Madrid, and then he had stayed to do some business. He sat Conchi on his knee and asked her the names of all her dolls. He listened to her chatter about the friends she had made across the street, and then he turned to Rafa to find out what he'd been up to.

Rafa asked him about the castle. 'Can we go and see it?' he said.

Uncle Fat shrugged. 'It's only a ruin. A few stones. Half the village was built with stones from the castle walls. There's nothing to see.'

So then Rafa asked him about the little house. 'Who does it belong to?' he wanted to know.

He was planning to go back there, in the hope of finding the dog again. Besides, he'd left his football there. He'd forgotten all about it until now.

'One of the neighbours,' Uncle Fat said. 'Nobody lives there. But you'd better keep out of it. Some kids were playing there once and they set it on fire. Almost burned up the whole cornfield.'

'There's a bed and a mattress – sort of,' said Rafa.

'Well maybe the shepherd sleeps there sometimes.'

'Does the shepherd have a dog?'

'Several, I expect. Why?'

Rafa was silent. He still hadn't got over Aunt Meri's attack on Moro. Perhaps Uncle Fat didn't like dogs, either.

Aunt Meri put in, 'He's thinking about that rogue, Moro. What do you think? I came back from the shop and he had him here, in this house, in this very kitchen.' Her voice rose higher and higher with indignation at every word.

Uncle Fat laughed.

'Trust Moro to take advantage of a city boy. He must have seen you coming, Rafa. Green as green.'

Rafa felt himself going red. He didn't like being told he was green, even though he knew Uncle Fat didn't mean to be unkind. But he was laughing at him.

'He was hungry. I only wanted to give him something to eat.'

'He's a thief, that's what he is,' said Aunt Meri.

'He didn't steal anything. I gave it to him,' Rafa protested.

'Moro's a gypsy,' said Uncle Fat. 'Beg or steal, it's all the same to him.'

'Who does he belong to?' asked Rafa.

'The devil!' came Aunt Meri's feeling reply.

'He belongs to himself does that one,' said Uncle Fat.

'Then how do you know his name?'

'Moro? Everyone calls him Moro. Because he's black, I suppose.'

'Black-haired and black-hearted,' said Aunt Meri.

'He's not black-hearted,' protested Rafa. 'He's really nice. And funny.'

'He's a bit of a rogue, but I suppose you have to be if everyone's against you,' conceded Uncle Fat. 'Me? I admire him.'

'Dogs are dirty things,' put in Conchi. 'And they eat you.'

Uncle Fat burst out laughing. 'And who's going to eat you, my little pet? If Moro so much as looks at you, I'll get out my gun and shoot him dead.'

37

'Oh, she's stupid,' said Rafa, scared that perhaps Uncle Fat would do just that if Moro came back.

'I'm not stupid. And you're bad because you went away and you didn't stay with me like Aunt Meri said.'

'Ninny,' sneered Rafa.

'Idiot!'

'Cry baby!'

'Enough! Enough!' laughed Uncle Fat. 'Let's forget about Moro and eat in peace.'

Aunt Meri was just putting soup in their dishes and both Rafa and Conchi fell silent, though they gave each other murderous looks across the table which the grown-ups either didn't notice, or ignored.

After the meal Aunt Meri made them have a siesta because it was far too hot to do anything but sleep. Rafa and Conchi were sharing a bed, something they had never done before. It was a huge bed – big enough for an elephant to sleep in, Papa had said when he tucked them in the night before – and Aunt Meri had put a long pillow down the middle so they wouldn't fight over whose side was whose.

They didn't talk to each other, still full of resentment. Rafa's head was aching a bit from so much sun, but although he shut his eyes he couldn't sleep. He kept thinking about Moro, wondering where he was and whether he was really as bad as Aunt Meri made out.

Suddenly Conchi pleaded, 'Tell me a story, Rafa.'

Rafa was silent.

'Please,' she said, after a while.

Rafa often told Conchi stories. It started when she was little, before she knew how to read. Mama bought Conchi cheap books in the market so she could look at the pictures and scribble in them, and Papa read the stories to her on his day off. But Papa wasn't often at home so Rafa started to read to her instead, Red Riding Hood, The Three Bears, Tom Thumb . . .

Then he started mixing the stories up to tease her, because she used to get cross when he didn't use the right words. But then she liked it and was always asking him for something new. The stories she liked best were the ones he made up about her dolls, except when they got killed falling out of aeroplanes, or squashed by underground trains. Rafa's stories were often very gory and they sometimes made her scream. And Mama would get cross, but really Conchi loved them.

'Tell me about Mari-Bel,' she begged. That was her favourite doll just now.

'Go to sleep,' was all Rafa said.

Silence for a few minutes. Then, 'Rafa . . .? Rafa, will you tell me a story about Moro?'

'Moro?' replied Rafa, in spite of himself.

'Yes . . . that dog. The one you like. Tell me a story about him.'

'But you don't like dogs.'

'I'm scared of them.'

'There's no reason to be, especially with Moro. He's so nice. So funny.'

'Tell me about him. I want to know.'

'Only if you promise to be nice to him.'

'I will. I will . . . if you're there with me. I won't be scared if you're there.'

'And tonight we'll go and look for him?'

'If you want to.'

'And you'll help me convince Aunt Meri he's not bad?'

'If you want.'

'And you won't scream?'

'I promise.'

'All right then,' agreed Rafa, satisfied at last. 'I'll tell you about him.'

But he almost didn't, because he started thinking about Moro again; how he met him in the little house, how Moro

39

had looked at him with such adoration and had licked him all over and jumped on him, and run backwards and forwards with him across the fields, and come into the house so bold and hungry . . .

'Rafa!' came the petulant reminder.

'O.K., O.K. I was just thinking. Let's see. Once upon a time . . .' Every story had to start like that.

'Once upon a time there was a little black dog and his name was Moro, and he lived in a little house, all by himself, because he didn't have a master and nobody cared about him. If he wanted to eat, he had to steal his food, and people got angry with him and chased him away.'

'Just like Aunt Meri?' said Conchi.

'Yes, just like Aunt Meri.'

'She was unkind,' Conchi went on.

'Yes, but she didn't understand. She didn't know he was hungry.'

'And why hasn't he died of hunger if he doesn't have anyone to feed him?'

'Ah!' exclaimed Rafa dramatically. 'That's because no one knew his secret.'

'What secret? What secret?' Conchi loved secrets.

'That, really, he was a prince in disguise.'

'Like the princess and the frog?'

'A bit, but not quite. He was an African prince. That's why he was black, and he lived in the castle up on the hill.'

'You said he lived in a little house.'

'Well, so he did. As a dog. But when he was a prince, he lived in the castle.'

'Is that the castle you asked Uncle Fat about?'

'Yes.'

'He said it's fallen down.'

'That's all he knows. And, anyway, who's telling this story? Why don't you shut up and listen.'

Conchi shut up and listened and Rafa told her how the

40

little dog had been bewitched for a thousand years, and how he had to find a family to love him if ever he was to become a prince again and restore the castle and go back and live there.

'But he has to steal to eat, so people hate him and nobody loves him, and that's why for a thousand years he's still a dog instead of a prince, and the castle's fallen down, and nobody cares.'

'You care,' said Conchi.

'Yes,' said Rafa.

'Why don't we have him? We could love him. We're a family. Then he could be a prince again and go back to his castle. That'd be lovely,' said Conchi. She gave a yawn. 'Why don't you tell Aunt Meri about him. Then she'll let you have him.'

'She won't,' disagreed Rafa.

'I'm going to tell her,' said Conchi. 'I want to have him.'

'It's got to be a secret,' argued Rafa. 'If you tell her, I bet we'll never find him again.'

'But if we do . . .?'

'Then we'll see,' said Rafa. 'We'll see.'

7

That evening Uncle Fat took everybody to the river. It wasn't very far away, only ten minutes in the car – going slowly, too, because it was only a cart track and Aunt Meri didn't like to be bounced.

On the way Uncle Fat stopped to pick up two boys going in the same direction with towels under their arms.

'Pepe! Victor!' he exclaimed in the hearty way all village people seemed to use.

They climbed into the back. Conchi had to sit on Aunt Meri's lap, and Uncle Fat put his arm round Rafa's shoulders as he went on in his loud voice, 'My nephew, Rafa, who's come to stay with us for a while with his sister Conchi.'

Rafa was glad he was in the front seat. Like that he didn't have to talk to the boys, and he couldn't see if they stared at him. He hated it when grown-ups expected you to be friendly with complete strangers, just because they happened to be about the same age as yourself.

Aunt Meri started telling Pepe and Victor all about him. Rafa wished she'd shut up, especially when she went on to say how she hoped they would be friends with him and look after him. At this, Rafa felt like curling up inside.

'Of course we'll look after him,' said Pepe, the elder of the two. Rafa didn't like the way he said it. There was mockery beneath the politeness.

To his relief Aunt Meri then started asking them about

their families and, by the time they'd answered all her questions, they'd arrived at the river bank and Uncle Fat had found a shady place beneath the trees to park the car.

It was a very wide river, with dark, deep water. In places there were big clumps of underwater plants and stretches of water lilies. In the middle of the river was a strong current. You could see how quickly broken branches floated down on it. There was a long, narrow beach where the bank sloped down to the water, but in most parts the bank was steep and high, especially on the far side. All the way along either bank were tall trees which broke the sunlight into dappled patterns on the water.

Boys were diving off the high bank, some with style, others just throwing themselves in with shouts of bravado, legs and arms spreadeagled. Splashes and cries drowned each other.

Rafa stood and stared. He was used to crowded swimming pools, and to splashing about in the rivers near Madrid, which never had much water in them and were full of rocks. But this was a river such as he had never seen before. No wonder Uncle Fat wanted to be sure he could swim before letting him come alone, and had gone on and on about the weeds, and the current, and the depth.

'Coming?' Pepe's challenge broke into his thoughts.

He and Victor had already pulled off their shirts and jeans. Their bodies were brown and sinewy. They helped with the work on the land and were almost as hard looking as Uncle Fat.

In his swimming trunks, Rafa felt very conscious of his pale skin. He couldn't help being a bit scared inside, remembering Papa's tales about village boys. Pepe and Victor were older than him, as well as looking so much stronger. But Uncle Fat and Aunt Meri were watching, so they couldn't really do him any harm.

The sun overhead was burning. The heat of the ground

43

crept right up his legs, and his whole body longed for the cool, dark water in spite of his qualms.

'Go on with you!' cried Aunt Meri, from where she was sitting under a tree, helping Conchi take off her dress. 'Let's see you in the water.'

'Wait for me,' cried Conchi. 'Wait for me. I want to go in the water, too.'

'Hurry up, then.'

Rafa and Aunt Meri took Conchi down to the water between them, Aunt Meri hitching up her skirt with one hand and paddling her corns – because it was good for them, she said. Conchi splashed about for a while, throwing water over Rafa and squealing when he threw it over her. Then she settled down on the beach to make mud pies for her dolls.

Rafa had forgotten about Pepe and Victor. They'd joined the boys higher up. Some of them were racing each other to the far bank and back again, while others shouted insults and encouragements.

Rafa found his depth and swam back and forth within it, not very far from Conchi and Aunt Meri. Then he started showing off for Conchi, diving under the water to bring up stones for her, seeing how long he could stay under. Gradually he went further away from the bank, closer to the middle, to the fast current, where the water ran cold and strong and challenging. Every time he felt the sun burning on his head, he dived under the water. It was the best way of keeping cool.

'Bet you can't cross!'

The voice came behind him. It was Pepe.

'My uncle's told me not to.'

'Bah! You're scared.'

'No I'm not.'

'Come on, then. I'll race you across. Bet you can't swim that far.'

44

'Oh yes I can. I've swum the whole length of the pool back home, an Olympic pool. That's twice as far.'

'Huh! Swimming pools! I'll race you tomorrow, when your uncle's not here.'

'I don't know if I'm coming tomorrow.'

'We all come here. What else are you going to do?'

'I don't know yet. I've got other plans.'

'I bet.'

Rafa wasn't going to tell Pepe about Moro, but he certainly intended to find Moro before he did anything else. And go back to the little house for his football.

His silence brought a triumphant leer to Pepe's wet face. The next second he felt his legs being kicked and caught up by Pepe's, and the more he struggled to free them, the more they were clamped by the other boy's.

'Let me go,' he shouted, and felt a great rush of water down his throat and up his nose as Pepe suddenly pulled him under.

The next few seconds were the longest in Rafa's life as he struggled to regain the surface, fighting off Pepe's hold, and choking, choking, lungs paralysed and feeling about to burst.

There was a sudden sensation of cold, gasping cold. The current! Panic exploded inside him and he fought like a wild thing, arms and legs thrashing, not even knowing where the surface was.

For seconds he was grasped by a swirling, utter loneliness that was like dying. Then his head shot out of the water. Sunlight burst upon his eyes. His mouth opened in great gasps but still he couldn't breathe or hear or see. Instinct alone kept him afloat.

Swim, swim, his brain was telling him, and suddenly he found he was using his arms and legs, and the bank was near . . . within reach . . . he was clinging to grass, roots . . . he was pulling himself up, sitting on dry ground, shivering,

45

shaking, almost crying.

Just a few yards away, still in the water, Victor and Pepe, with a crowd of other boys, were watching him and laughing.

On the way back home in the car, an hour later, Uncle Fat said jovially to Rafa, 'Well, I think you can swim well enough. You'll be able to come here whenever you want with the other boys. What a wonderful way to spend the summer! I tell you, you won't have time to be bored.'

Rafa just looked out of the window and said nothing.

8

'When are we going to look for Moro?' demanded Conchi at suppertime. She'd already forgotten it was supposed to be a secret.

Rafa gave her a black look, and she made things worse by throwing her hands across her mouth, eyes round with contrition.

Aunt Meri looked from one to the other.

'What are you two up to?' she asked, more amused than suspicious. Conchi's face was a picture of guilt.

'Nothing,' said Rafa. 'We just thought if we had nothing else to do we'd see if we could find Moro again.'

'That dog! You just forget about him. Before you know what's what, he'll be worming his way in here and making off with everything, lock, stock and barrel.'

Rafa couldn't help grinning at the prospect. Moro was a very 'wormy' sort of dog, wriggling and curling all over the place.

'But he's a good dog,' coaxed Conchi. 'Rafa says he's really a prince.'

'That Moro's no storybook dog. He's a rogue and a thief.'

Conchi's eyes stared back unbelievingly at Aunt Meri. 'But Rafa says . . .' she went on insistently.

'And what does Rafa say?' interrupted Uncle Fat teasingly. 'I think that brother of yours tells you some tall stories.'

'All sorts,' agreed Conchi happily, not understanding what he meant. 'He says that really Moro –'

'It was only a story,' Rafa shut her up. 'Just to make her go to sleep.'

'But that rogue of a dog has already got at you, I can see that,' said Uncle Fat. 'Now he's becoming a legend, and all in a day!'

'Uncle Fat . . .' began Conchi in a wheedling tone. She pushed her hand into his.

Rafa knew all the signs. She was the best wheedler he'd ever come across, knew exactly how to get what she wanted. Sometimes it made him sick, but he also had to admit that Conchi's wheedling had its uses.

'Uncle Fat,' repeated Conchi. 'If we can find him again, can we have him? Can he be ours?'

'Listen to the child!' exclaimed Aunt Meri with astonishment. 'You've got more than enough dolls, half the dolls from the shops of Madrid. What do you want with a dog?'

'To play with. Rafa says he's fun. Rafa wants him. And I want him. Can we have him? Please say yes, Uncle Fat. I'll love you for ever if you do.'

'Who can resist such a promise?' laughed Uncle Fat. 'I'll get you the moon if you promise to love me for ever,' and he gave her such a hard kiss that she squealed and said his whiskers had scratched her skin.

That made him laugh even more, and he began teasing her in earnest, rubbing his chin on her arm and cheek until Aunt Meri sharply called both of them to order.

After supper they had to dress in their best clothes to go for a stroll round the village. Uncle Fat and Aunt Meri wanted to show Rafa and Conchi off to everybody. Conchi adored being the centre of attention, so she didn't mind. She spent twenty minutes deciding which doll to take with her, although Rafa knew all along that she'd choose Mari-Bel, her Christmas doll. It could walk when you put batteries in its stomach, and say, 'Mama', but the batteries were always running out and Mama hadn't bought any new ones for a long time.

Rafa wasn't so keen on being on show, especially when Conchi went ahead with Uncle Fat, chattering to him, lapping up his flattery and affection, leaving him to Aunt Meri, who walked much slower and talked to him as if he were no older than Conchi.

They passed through the village square, where a tall church rose up against the moonlight, proud and dark. On top of its square bell tower, the sticks of a stork's nest poked out untidily.

'Look!' Rafa heard Uncle Fat exclaim to Conchi, pointing upwards. 'That's where the stork lives. He'll be bringing you a baby brother or sister very soon now.'

'Mama says our baby's coming from Paris,' argued Conchi.

'Yes? Well, perhaps our stork only brings *our* babies.'

'How? How?' insisted Conchi, tugging at her uncle's hand.

His laughter rolled out across the square. Rafa didn't hear him answer because just then Aunt Meri said, 'We'll go to mass on Sunday to pray for your Mama.'

'Nothing's going to happen to her!'

His reply was almost a shout. He had forgotten his fears until his aunt's remark suddenly brought them back.

'Well of course not. But it's always good to pray – that she won't have a bad time. That the baby will be healthy.'

Rafa made no reply. His heart was beating fast, like it had when he first thought Mama was going to die. It made him dizzy. Papa had promised, but . . .

Oh, if only he could have stayed at home and seen that Mama was all right! If only he weren't here, in the village. He'd be with his friends. He could talk about it with them. Most of their mothers had babies from time to time. It was

49

better talking about it with your friends. Grown-ups never explained things properly. Either they didn't want you to know and got embarrassed and angry about it, or they supposed you knew everything anyway and only left you puzzled.

Having a baby was the biggest mystery Rafa could imagine. Once Mama put his hand on her stomach when the baby was moving inside her and Rafa felt it lurch at his touch. What was moving? A leg? An arm? What was the baby doing in there? Stretching? Turning round? It was alive all right, and yet . . . Most of the time it didn't seem real.

Most of the time he didn't even think about it, not as you think about a real person. Did it sleep and wake up the same as he did? Was it asleep all the time? And how could there be enough room?

He thought about these things when he sat on the little kitchen balcony at home, the same way as he sometimes looked up at the stars and wondered about them. Were there people, or some kind of people, on any other planet? Did they wonder about him as he wondered about them? Where was God? All these things were mysteries, but they were all far away mysteries. This baby was so close and frightening sometimes that he could hardly breathe.

Disco music suddenly blaring to life woke him from his thoughts. There was a brightly lit café at the end of the street, with a garden beside for which everybody seemed to be making. Uncle Fat shepherded them in and found a table not too close to the music. Everything was cool and damp. A boy with a hose pipe was still watering the ground, now and again squirting it over a crowd of youngsters who were deliberately taunting him with this aim in view.

Coloured lights were strung between the trees, against which moths burned their wings and fell helpless to the ground. Hordes of mosquitoes shimmered in the same light. Waiters rushed around, slapping down drinks and snacks, shouting out new orders, half in darkness, half in light. The brightest place was the tiled area where a few people were already dancing. A spotlight on a tall pole beamed right over them and over all the surrounding tables.

Suddenly, there were shouts and laughter as into the spotlight, right across the centre of the dancing area and with no respect for its purpose, confidently trotted a thin, black dog. He stopped in the middle, looking from one dancer to another, probably wondering what strange things they were up to but knowing it had nothing to do with him.

'It's Moro!' exclaimed Rafa, jumping up from his chair.

Other people had jumped up with similar exclamations and already several lads were after him, closing in on him across the dance floor, bodies low, hands ready to grab, the dancing, but not the music, momentarily suspended.

Moro stood stock still in the centre, wary, taut, instinct and experience telling him where each one was without needing to use his eyes. The boys waited for him to make a move, clicking impatiently when he did nothing, or slapping their legs.

Moro knew they wanted some fun. He was feeling full of beans himself after one of the biggest meals he'd had for ages, thanks to Rafa. There was the showman's instinct in him. Perhaps the atmosphere, the lights, the music, people laughing and shouting, kids screeching and getting wet, all had its effect on him. Perhaps he just knew he was the centre of attention, under that glaring light, and really liked it.

Whatever he thought or felt – and who can ever know what any dog thinks or feels, supposing it can do either of these things? – Moro decided to give the lads a run instead of dashing for the thicket of table legs and chairs, and the safety of puddles and darkness.

Yapping out his challenge to them, he began rushing

51

around within the circle of their hands, dodging with practised skill as first one and then another lunged after him. He dashed between their legs and barked scornfully at their backsides, darting back again even as they turned with swear words and surprise.

Everyone was laughing and shouting encouragement and advice, both for the boys and Moro, and there was a great roar as someone tripped over Moro and landed flat on his back.

'I'll kill you,' Rafa heard the boy rage, as he came after Moro again with deadly intent. And then Rafa recognized him. It was Pepe.

'First you got to catch him,' someone shouted back at him, and for what seemed ages to Rafa, Pepe chased round after the little black dog, growing more and more furious while Moro's yaps grew more and more hysterical.

Rafa stood there frozen. At first he had laughed with everyone else – Moro was the clown of clowns and no mistake – but soon he was aware that what had started as fun had become deadly earnest and that if Moro was caught...

'Escape, escape,' he pleaded mentally with Moro. Didn't the silly dog know the danger he was in? 'Oh, please run away,' he begged.

'Is that Moro? Is that Moro?' Conchi was shouting in his ear, tugging at his shirt because he didn't answer.

And suddenly Moro wasn't there any more. He'd run his pursuers into confusion on the dance floor, all to the tune of 'Saturday Night Fever', and had dived out of the spotlight into the darkness beyond. A couple of chairs went flying, there were a few shouts, and a single yelp – had somebody kicked him? – but Moro had melted into the blackness. He'd had enough.

Rafa sat down. His knees were trembling and his shirt was stuck to his back. Uncle Fat was laughing away while Aunt

Meri made disapproving noises about 'that dog'. Conchi was saying, 'He's so funny, isn't he? Isn't he sweet?' She hadn't understood at all.

And Rafa felt very strange, different to everybody else.

9

Rafa soon realized he needn't have worried about finding Moro again. Although the little dog had vanished from the crowded café garden as rapidly as he had disappeared from the street earlier in the day, the next morning his was the first face Rafa saw when he stepped out into the street after breakfast.

Aunt Meri had said he was like a bad penny, 'always turning up,' and it seemed she was right.

The moment Moro saw Rafa he jumped to his feet (he was lying in the shadow of the neighbour's house across the street) and began to wag his tail. Conchi was with Rafa. Her first reaction was to cling to him tightly, ready to scream.

'Silly!' he told her. 'It's Moro. Have you forgotten him already?'

'Are you sure he won't hurt me?' she begged, her self-confidence completely gone.

'Of course he won't hurt you. Look, you just stay in the doorway and watch. Then you'll see how friendly he is.'

Conchi did as she was told, back pressing against the door. She watched Rafa cross the street, one hand outstretched as he made clicking noises with his tongue. For a moment it looked as though Moro was going to dash away – he was all tensed up, which made his thin tail wag even faster – and he did look so funny; fearful and joyful at the same time. He was making little whimpering noises in his throat.

Just as Rafa was about to touch him, Moro dashed away, but not very far. He went berserk, dashing round and round in circles, running up to Rafa then running away again, but not for a second letting the boy touch him.

'He's crazy!' exclaimed Conchi, forgetting to be afraid. And she began to laugh.

Rafa knew Moro was scared. This was just how he acted yesterday, in the house. He knew Moro wanted to be friends, was longing to be friends, and so he just stood there, waiting for Moro to calm down.

'Shut up,' he shouted at Conchi. 'You're frightening him.'

Conchi shut up.

'Go and ask Aunt Meri if we can give him something to eat,' Rafa told her. 'And be quick, in case he runs away.'

Conchi ran to the kitchen, face flushed with excitement. Aunt Meri was sitting at the table, sorting out spotted beans for a stew.

'Aunt Meri, give me something to eat for Moro. He's outside and Rafa says to bring him something to eat.'

'Does he now? And what have I said about that dog?'

'Oh, go on. Uncle said we can have Moro if we want him. Don't you remember? Just to play with. We won't bring him in. Come on . . . Just a little, weeny bit of something. A weeny, weeny bit . . .'

Conchi was an artist at getting what she wanted. Her dark eyes grew big with longing, almost with pain.

'We're so lonely here without our friends. If we had Moro to play with . . .'

'Nonsense!' exclaimed Aunt Meri. 'Whoever heard of playing with a dog?' but she was already getting up from the table and going towards the larder, sighing with disapproval.

'That dog! I don't suppose I've got anything. Maybe some bread and milk. I'll look in the rubbish. We had those lamb chops last night. I expect the bones are still there.'

'Oh, you're so good and kind, Aunt, and I'm going to give

you a big kiss!' exclaimed Conchi, throwing her arms round her aunt's waist.

Conchi frowned with care as she carried the bowl of bread and milk in her hands, not wanting Moro to lose a single drop.

'Rafa, Rafa,' she called, very pleased with herself, and pleased for Moro, too.

They were just inside the archway, out of the sun. It looked as if they were having a fight. Rafa was half lying down and Moro was half on top of him, tongue out, white teeth gleaming, making horrible growly noises.

Conchi gave a scream and dropped the bowl as she dashed back to Aunt Meri, yelling that Rafa was being eaten alive. The crash of the bowl, the bread and milk splashing in all directions, put Moro in full flight. One moment he was there, the next he had gone.

Aunt Meri came charging out with a broom in her hands and there was Rafa picking himself up, looking as angry as he felt.

'My sister's the biggest idiot ever,' he cried.

'You see, you see,' exclaimed Aunt Meri. 'I knew no good could come of having that Moro around.'

'But, Aunt,' whined Conchi. 'I really thought Rafa . . . that he was going to be eaten.'

'Dogs don't eat people,' Rafa yelled at her, face black with fury. 'When are you going to stop being so stupid? When are you going to grow up?'

'Don't talk to your sister like that!' Aunt Meri shouted at him. 'She was really scared for you. And that's the second bowl broken since yesterday, and all for that gypsy dog.

'It was Conchi's fault. She dropped it,' muttered Rafa as he bent down to pick up the pieces.

'Leave it. Leave it. Next thing you'll be cutting yourself. Now go off and play somewhere, and forget about that dog. Go and find your football. Conchi can stay here with me.'

Sulkily, Rafa went off down the street. He'd hardly turned the corner when Moro came dancing up to him, barking round him with joy, fear forgotten.

'Come on,' Rafa shouted to him, as he broke into a run. And Moro loped along beside him, sometimes jumping up, sometimes yapping.

They ran through all the village without stopping, past mule carts, old women in black, and small children playing in doorways, and they ran down the middle of the street because there weren't any cars or lorries or contamination to bother them. And then they collapsed together at the roadside, crushing the stiff summer grass, and went on with the battle that Conchi had interrupted so disastrously. When they were worn out from that, they just sat and looked at each other, panting and grinning, the best of friends.

Later, they went back to the little house together, to collect Rafa's football. It was still there. Moro jumped up on the mattress and chased about on it for a while, tearing new holes in it, urged on by Rafa's laughter. Then he found something to chew and stopped playing.

It was a hoof paring and he very cleverly held it between his front paws as he gnawed at one end. Rafa started to stroke him, but eating was a serious business and Moro slunk under the bed with his food and didn't reappear until he'd choked down the last morsel.

At the time, Rafa didn't know what Moro was eating – not until a few days later when, in Moro's company, he watched the blacksmith shoe someone's horse, and Moro started chewing up the parings.

'Won't it hurt him!' he exclaimed to the blacksmith, when he threw the first bit at Moro's feet.

'Beggars can't be choosers,' was the blacksmith's reply. 'Anyway, he's always coming here for what he can find and, up till now . . .'

But, before then, when Rafa saw how Moro chewed

hungrily on that bit of hard, grey stuff, he remembered the smashed bowl of bread and milk which would have been Moro's breakfast. And he took Moro back home again, sure that Aunt Meri would have forgotten her anger by then.

She had, and the chop bones were still in the newspaper, under the sink in the patio. Conchi brought them out to Rafa, as he sat in the doorway with Moro, not daring to leave him, not daring to take him any further.

Conchi thought she was being very brave, getting so close to Moro, especially when he began to look at her with a very hungry look, and sniff the air excitedly because suddenly he knew that whatever was in the roll of paper was for him.

'Don't be scared,' insisted Rafa as she stopped dead, staring at Moro. 'He won't hurt you. He's just hungry, that's all. Here!'

He jumped up, took the packet from her and stuck it under Moro's nose. Moro wriggled with excitement from the tip of his nose to the last limp curl in his tail. He began whining and jumping up.

'Give it to him, give it to him,' cried Conchi, half scared, half longing to see him eat.

Rafa put the package on the ground. Moro's nose was between the pages almost before Rafa could unwrap them. And the two children watched, not without surprise, as the hungry dog snapped and crunched his way through the pile of bones, hardly pausing to swallow. It looked quite a painful business, the way Moro screwed his face up, half shutting his eyes. Odd splinters fell onto the paper and Moro licked them up.

'Cor!' said Conchi with great feeling. She was squatting on her haunches not too far away, eyes round with amazement.

Rafa just grinned with contentment. Who could have guessed there could be so much pleasure just watching a hungry dog eat?

10

Moro knew when he was on to a good thing.

Aunt Meri hadn't summed up his nature fairly when she had called him a black-hearted rogue because, really, there wasn't an ounce of badness in him. But the very life he lived had taught him how to take advantage of every situation, or he would never have survived so long.

Moro lived from moment to moment. He had learned enough of human nature not to be puzzled by anything people did, good or bad. He quickly worked out that Rafa liked him, that Rafa wasn't going to hurt him, that there was food forthcoming from Rafa's hands.

So Moro was outside the door where Rafa lived, day after day, waiting. Perhaps there was more hope than usual in his waiting – because each day Rafa gave him more reason to hope, to expect – but if sometimes Rafa failed him, it didn't upset him. He'd go away for a while on some other business, then come back and start waiting again.

If Rafa had known more about dogs like Moro, he wouldn't have been so anxious whenever the little dog didn't happen to be around. He didn't know about the hours Moro waited patiently in some place where he could keep an eye or an ear on Rafa's house, unrewarded hours spent dozing and scratching. All Rafa knew was that when he ran out of the house to look for Moro, sometimes he was there and sometimes he wasn't.

When he was there Moro would leap up to him, eyes

bright, tail furiously wagging, panting with excitement and joy. And there was real devotion in Moro's greeting because he was ready to hand out instant love to anyone who'd accept it.

Rafa really liked that. There's something special about being greeted by a dog that goes wild with joy at the sight of you. It makes you feel good, especially when the dog isn't really yours, and you've got a guilty conscience because yesterday you forgot to find any food for him.

Moro never took it badly when Rafa had nothing for him to eat. He loved him just the same, licked him all over, was ready to go with him anywhere – even on an empty stomach. Moro wasn't used to eating much, anyway, and he was as much satisfied by Rafa's company as by his food.

Both Rafa and Conchi did their best to keep him fed. It was just that sometimes Aunt Meri had no leftovers to give him. When they had steak, for example. There were never any leftovers from steak and chips, and Aunt Meri cooked them steak quite often because it was the most expensive meat at the butcher's and therefore it had to be good for them.

'We must tell her we only want chicken or chops,' Rafa said to Conchi, thinking of all the bones that would be left over. 'And if we always leave some bits on our plates . . . We don't have to eat everything,' he said.

'But I like steak,' argued Conchi selfishly. They didn't have it very often at home.

'Well, I hope it chokes you,' was Rafa's angry reply.

Leftover beans or lentils or rice were always given to Aunt Meri's chickens, which she kept up on the roof, and Rafa couldn't persuade her to let Moro have a share.

'I get eggs from the hens,' she told him. 'What do I get from that vagabond except broken dishes?'

One day Rafa went shopping with Aunt Meri. At the poulterer's he saw neat little piles of head, claws and gizzard, which people bought to make soup. They were the same price as five bubble gums. Rafa knew Aunt Meri would complain if he spent his pocket money on food for Moro, so he went back later on his own. After that, at least twice a week he bought chicken bits for Moro.

The man in the shop was puzzled because Aunt Meri had never made so many chicken soups before. When Rafa told him they were for Moro, who waited outside the door, black nose sometimes poking through the bead curtains, the man roared with laughter. But sometimes he would thrust a whole pile of chicken claws into Rafa's hands and not take any money for them.

Moro cracked them up a little between his jaws, but swallowed them whole. Sometimes it looked as though they wouldn't go down. They stuck in his throat. But in the end he managed.

'Moro's like a dustbin,' Conchi said once, watching him struggle with a bit of pig's ear, curled up with age, that he'd found somewhere, and Rafa grinned in agreement. There wasn't anything he wouldn't eat, even shoe leather.

People began to get used to seeing Moro hang about outside Aunt Meri's house, or following Rafa along to the poulterer's and the baker's, and to Uncle Fat's yard, where he was building a new house.

Uncle Fat was in the building trade, as well as being a farmer. He built houses for other people, and now he was building new one for himself, a really modern home. 'But perhaps I'll give it to my son and daughter,' he said when Rafa asked him why he wanted to have two houses when the one he had already was very big.

He let Rafa help him. He showed him how to make cement and how to splash water over it on the walls, to stop it drying too soon in the heat. He told him all about drainage and electricity, because Uncle Fat understood a lot about these things, too, although he did have two men

61

helping him. Rafa carried bricks and tiles and generally messed about, and wherever he went, Moro ran about behind him, poking his nose into everything and covering himself in brick dust and cement powder.

There was an old donkey in Uncle Fat's yard, the very same one that Rafa had fallen off all those years ago. Uncle Fat said Ana was twenty years old.

'What does she do?' Rafa wanted to know.

'Nothing now. I'm waiting for her to die, but blow me if she's not determined to live for ever.'

Ana was a very unfriendly donkey. She wandered about at the end of a rope, nibbling up tough bits of grass filmed with dust, and when Rafa tried to get near to her to say hello, she kicked or tried to bite him. She wasn't like that with Uncle Fat, though. She let him put his arm round her. Perhaps that was because every night he gave her a big bucket of barley and chaff.

Uncle Fat kept teasing him, 'Want a ride? Want a ride?'

Rafa stopped trying to get friendly with Ana after she'd kicked Moro in the ribs one day, just because he happened to be following rat trails through the rubble and thistles. Moro let out a chorus of yelps that made Rafa's blood run cold, and when Rafa got hold of him to see where he was hurt, Moro in fear and pain tried to bite his hands.

'Leave him alone,' shouted one of the workmen who was watching. 'It'll take more than old Ana to put paid to him, and what will your aunt say if he bites you?'

Moro eventually went to sleep with his head across Rafa's legs, Rafa stroking his hard black skull, and the two of them stayed still together for a long time, in spite of the way the men joked about them both. And when Moro woke up he was as good as new, tail wagging, paws dancing, tongue slobbering everywhere, his jaws never closed.

And Moro had every reason to wag his tail and dance about, because in some subtle fashion his status in the village had improved. He was still 'that rogue Moro', 'that gypsy', 'that vagabond', but now his name was frequently connected with Rafa's; he belonged to Rafa as much as he would ever 'belong' to anyone; and this gave him a certain amount of respectability he hadn't had since he first came to the village with the mattress man.

Perhaps people felt that if he was with Rafa, and Rafa was feeding him and looking after him, he wouldn't be so keen to sneak into their houses to steal. And when people saw Conchi playing with him, when they saw Moro carrying her dolls on his back and Conchi running along beside him, holding them up, laughing with joy, they thought that perhaps Moro had some good in him after all.

Even the boys found they could have as much fun playing with Moro as teasing him. They discovered he was a first-class footballer. This was because Rafa had started playing games with Moro with his football. At first, when Rafa threw the ball to him, Moro was scared and ran off, thinking Rafa wanted to hurt him with it.

He stayed at a distance – watching Rafa dribbling the ball along with his toe, bouncing it, heading it – his dark eyes curious, puzzled, his dog brain taking it all in. Suddenly, he darted back to Rafa, barking madly, bravely, challenging the black and white ball that stood between them. Gently, Rafa pushed it towards him and Moro pounced . . .

That was just the beginning. Conchi would be in fits of laughter at the things Moro got up to with that ball. He tried to pick it up with his teeth; he became an expert dribbler with his nose, driving it before him without losing it once, faster and faster where the ground was flat. He jumped on it, got his legs round it, and if it was sailing through the air, he would make tremendous leaps, sometimes managing to bring it down.

Soon not a football match could take place between a group of boys without Moro getting involved, and after that the boys would start arguing about whose side Moro was going to play for. Everyone wanted him on their side. Everyone wanted the fun of kicking the ball in his direction and seeing what he'd do with it. No one wanted the embarrassment of having a good shot interrupted by the other side's canine player.

Not that Moro took sides. He'd push the ball into his own goal as well as the other with equal willingness. So he could be a handicap, too. But none of the boys minded, although they argued a lot about whether Moro's scored goals counted or not.

But when the game was over, no matter how many boys were willing to pat him and make a fuss of him, or share their snacks with him, Moro stayed with Rafa (though he never refused the titbits), and trotted home with him.

He'd have to wait a long time in the street for something to eat – Aunt Meri wouldn't allow him even as far as the patio – before Rafa and Conchi came out with the scraps left over from supper. (Uncle Fat was in the conspiracy now of leaving something on his plate for Moro.) The neighbours got used to seeing him there, his black form growing shadowy in the gathering darkness, expectant but patient.

Where he spent the night, nobody knew, but Rafa sometimes dreamed of having Moro in bed with him, just like Papa did with his little white dog before it disappeared.

11

Moro was the boldest of dogs but there was one thing he was scared of. Water. This the boys discovered when Moro started going with them to the river. He'd never done it before Rafa came along but, these days, wherever Rafa went Moro was usually not far behind.

And the boys accepted him as they accepted Rafa. If one or two had wanted to be cruel to him, Moro now had Rafa to defend him. They were all boys about Rafa's own age – some were even related to him in one way or another – and with his easy-going nature, and their natural curiosity about him, it didn't take them all long to become friends.

Pepe went around with a gang of his own, so Rafa didn't see much of him, and generally speaking the two different age groups kept to their own stretch of the river if they happened to be there at the same time.

The river soon became as favourite a place for Rafa as it was for all the others. There, you could escape from the heat for as long as you liked, and eat bread and cheese under the trees, and not have any grown-ups around to bother you. It was better than the picnics Rafa was used to having with his parents. And there wasn't any day-trippers' rubbish around.

The first time Moro went along with them, Rafa forgot all about him just as soon as he was in the water. He only remembered him when he heard Moro's shrill barks from the bank.

'Come on in,' he yelled to him, and all the boys took up his cry.

'Moro! Come on in. Come on.'

Moro barked all the more hysterically, tail wagging wildly. He ran nervously along the bank, keeping up with them, but no matter how they called he didn't join them. Not even his anxiety to be near Rafa would persuade him to wet so much as the tips of his paws. Brave as Moro was about most things, he was an abject coward when it came to water. When the boys started splashing him, to their surprise he shot off with his tail between his legs, yelping with fear.

Hoots of scornful laughter followed after him.

'Let's get him,' someone shouted, scrambling out of the water.

'Leave him alone,' said Rafa fiercely.

They were used to Rafa defending Moro now, and so they left him alone. He was already out of sight, anyway. So they forgot about him and very soon Moro was back.

Rafa saw him under a tree, watching them all with pricked ears, both anxious and longing, not wanting to leave them, wanting to be part of the fun they were having, but too scared to join in. What a funny dog he was!

Rafa soon forgot him, just like the other boys, and when at last he clambered out of the water, tired out, he was both surprised and gratified when Moro came wheedling up to him in that wormy, half-scared, half-apologetic but eternally hopeful way of his, to lick his wet fingers and to jump over him with delight just as soon as Rafa was dressed and Moro knew he wasn't going back into the water again.

Moro always knew when the boys were going to the river, partly because they usually went in the early evening – and Moro's time-keeping was as good as theirs – but mostly because of their towels. Even though he hated the river, he always went along with them and sat under a tree, waiting for them to go home again.

One particular evening Pepe and his gang turned up looking for trouble. They started by kicking everyone's clothes into the water.

'Out of it, you kids,' shouted Pepe.

A pair of sandals smacked into the current and promptly sank, so everyone scrambled for the bank, grabbing at shirts and towels before they floated too far downstream and hoping to rescue their footwear, scattered beneath the trees. When Moro saw Rafa on firm ground again, he came dancing round him in his usual way, barking his relief and joy.

The next second he was swung in the air, tightly in the grip of Pepe's strong hands.

'Let's see if our star footballer is a good swimmer, too!' Pepe exclaimed, and there was a great splash as Moro hit the water and disappeared.

His black head bobbed up a second later, eyes looking round with frantic expression.

'Moro, Moro,' the younger boys chorused with Rafa. 'This way. This way.'

Moro began paddling for the bank as fast as possible. He certainly could swim! Rafa felt quite proud of him, in spite of his burning indignation against Pepe. But before Moro could scrabble to shore, another of Pepe's crowd was in the water, waiting for him.

He was grabbed and tossed back, and this time Moro disappeared right in the centre of the current. When his head bobbed up again he was already a good way further down from where he'd been thrown.

This time it was the older boys who called out, 'Moro. Moro.' It was a taunt, a challenge, and the dog in the water was as aware as Rafa was of their lack of sympathy.

Only Moro didn't understand it like that. To Moro, lack of sympathy was the pack instinct to get in and finish off your opponent when he was down. Survival lay only in fighting back, not hoping for pity. In this, Moro was exactly like his tormentors. Neither he nor they knew what pity was.

Rafa watched the little dog struggle against the current – swept along like a piece of driftwood, eyes wild with fear and effort – and the memory of his own panic when Pepe had pulled him under, and the current had gripped him, kept him frozen and helpless and silent.

There was a loud cheer as Moro broke free from the current and began paddling towards the bank again. He was away downstream, but his tormentors ran to keep abreast of him. Pepe was out front, ready to grab him just as soon as Moro's scrabbling feet were about to feel solid ground.

Moro somehow dodged, and Pepe plunged into the water after him, splashing, shouting threats. He got hold of Moro's tail, but let go with an oath as the dog snapped hysterically and caught his fingers. He grabbed Moro's legs, pulled him out of the water and tossed him with all his might back into the current again.

'Drown yourself once and for all,' Pepe shouted, face ugly with rage.

His words, his feeling, fell like a bane over everyone. With sinister curiosity, all eyes were turned on Moro's struggle out there, midstream. They were a long way now from where they always swam, where the village men had cleared the weeds to make it safe for them. It was Moro's last hour, they were sure of that. How long could he last? How soon would he give up? How quickly would the water take him?

The younger boys stared at Rafa, whose face was pale beneath his sun-reddened cheeks. He didn't see them because he was staring at Pepe's bronzed and powerful back as he waited half in the water, ready to grab poor Moro again, should he escape the current.

Then something seemed to burst in Rafa's head. An absolute passion of rage overwhelmed him. He flung

68

himself on Pepe from behind, half throttling him with the grip he got round his neck with his arm, before crashing into the water with him, when all became a haze of noise and pain that was never afterwards to be clear in his mind.

What happened was later to be talked about for weeks. It was a story that took time to tell, with many interruptions and embellishments, and it was one of the best battles they'd had in ages, Rafa's friends declared.

Stones had flown. One of the older boys had knocked himself out against a tree, chasing little Santi who, next to Moro, was the best dodger of them all. He had to have four stitches put in his head. ('Not that it'll do his brains any harm, because he never had any to start with.')

Pepe had somehow got a black eye, but no one could really swear it was Rafa who'd given it to him, and all of them had bruises and cuts they could proudly display. Rafa's scrap with Pepe had given him a cut lip, a swollen nose and a bruise on his cheek, all of which were painful for days.

But the biggest pain of all was the one Rafa carried secretly in his heart because Moro had disappeared and no one knew what had happened to him. Who knew where the indifferent river had taken him, while the boys attacked each other like savages over his fate? While everyone's blood was up Moro had been completely forgotten, and the younger boys had had to flee, anyway (even though they talked as if they'd won the battle). Only when they were back in the village, breathless, shaken, worn out, did Rafa realize that Moro wasn't with them. But, just then, there was no going back.

Aunt Meri had taken ice cubes out of the fridge, wrapped them in a cloth and made Rafa hold them to his nose to stop it bleeding, while she scolded and scolded, not listening to a word about Moro, except to say, 'That good-for-nothing dog! I told you from the start he was a trouble-maker. What would your mother say, if she saw you this minute? And her in hospital, having the baby!'

Rafa jumped up, startled. This was the first he'd heard of it.

'Is Mama having the baby?' he cried, his voice sounding muffled through his swollen nose.

'Your Papa rang up a couple of hours ago. He's going to ring again tonight, or whenever it's over. Now stick that thing back on your nose.'

'Is she all right?' Rafa wanted to know, heart racing anew with agitation.

Aunt Meri thought he was still overexcited about the fight. She pushed him back in the chair without any sympathy.

'Of course she'll be all right. No thanks to you, though. I don't wonder she wanted you out of the way.'

She wouldn't let him go to look for Moro. She was angry and worked up, and only calmed down when she'd shouted all her anger out at him. She made him sit and watch television and for a whole hour he was on his own, staring with unseeing eyes at the black and white figures so absolutely unreal, while his heart burned with anguish, both for Mama and for Moro.

It was after midnight when Papa rang again. The baby was born and Mama was just fine. Happy and just fine. The baby was a girl. They were going to call her Amparo because they'd all prayed to the Virgin of Amparo for her safe arrival. Amparo meant protection or refuge and everyone thought it was a very proper name for the new arrival.

Conchi, who was half asleep, kept asking complainingly, 'She's not going to be as pretty as me, is she, Aunt Meri?'

'Surely you're not jealous of your baby sister already?' exclaimed Aunt Meri, and Conchi burst into tears.

'I want to go home,' she sobbed. 'I want my Mama.'

'You'll be going home soon now,' Aunt Meri told her consolingly. 'You'll see. Just as soon as your Mama is strong enough.'

Conchi was asleep almost before Aunt Meri had tucked the sheet under her chin, too tired even for a story. Rafa was awake a while longer, thinking over all Papa had said on the phone.

He hadn't said much. He never did because he had to use a pay phone and he was always very conscious of the money being swallowed up, coin by coin. But he'd sounded very confident, excited and happy.

Rafa had never had the chance to tell him about Moro. Every time Papa phoned he'd wanted to, but there was never time. And he hadn't told Mama when she phoned from the neighbour's house, because she didn't like dogs and might tell him not to have anything to do with them.

And now Moro was gone. Perhaps the river had drowned him. And nobody really cared, except him. Of course he was glad about Mama, though the sick feeling which had come over him when Aunt Meri first told him she was in hospital still hadn't altogether left him, but . . .

He drifted off to sleep with a pain in his heart.

12

Rafa slept deeply that night. It wasn't till he woke up the next morning and tried to grin at Conchi, splitting open his cut lip, that all that had happened came back to him in a rush.

He jumped out of bed, pulled on his shorts and ran straight out to the street to see if Moro was waiting outside. But there was only the sun, harshly glaring, which made him screw up his eyes and reminded him of the tenderness of his nose. More slowly he went back to the kitchen and sat dully at the table, not even replying to Aunt Meri's greeting.

'What are you going to do with yourself today?' she asked him cheerily, though not without sympathy, seeing how glum he looked. She set a bowl of coffee and a plateful of cakes on the table in front of him.

Rafa heavily helped himself to three spoonfuls of sugar and stirred and stirred. He didn't look at his aunt. He knew she wouldn't understand how he felt.

'I'm going to look for Moro,' he said.

'That dog!' she sighed, but then she left him because Conchi was calling her.

That morning Rafa walked for ages along the river bank, in both directions. He was on his own and the river seemed a different place without the shouts of all the boys.

In spite of his anxiety, he was struck by the silent beauty of it all – the rows of trees with their thin, silvery trunks and silvery green leaves; the busyness of the ants who lived in a universe of their own, quite unaware of Rafa's existence. He had this strange sensation of being like God, walking among their scurryings and hurryings, and they not seeing him because he was so big, and because they never looked up.

Beyond the gaps in the trees there were glimpses of gold brown fields of stubble, and above his head was the intense blue of a cloudless sky. The sun was always with him, dancing on the small ripples of the water, shimmering on the leaves, melting horizons.

Aunt Meri had made him wear one of Uncle Fat's straw hats. He hadn't wanted to. It made him look like a bumpkin, he thought, but now he was glad he was wearing it, even though it made his forehead itch.

His eyes ached from looking at the river, roaming from bank to bank, trying to see into dark, overgrown holes. Once his heart leapt with sick recognition as he saw, just too far ahead to distinguish clearly, a black, bedraggled shape, half in, half out of the water. Not till he was close, his heart thumping painfully against his ribs, did he realize it was a big plastic bag. He picked it up and threw it into the river with relief.

He turned for home, tired, disheartened, sure he would never see Moro again. But the thought that the little dog might just be waiting for him when he got back took some of the weariness out of his legs. Moro wasn't there.

Uncle Fat tried to give him some comfort at lunchtime. 'We'll get in the car,' he said, 'and run round the lanes for a while. Maybe he swam across the river and can't find his way home.'

New hope filled Rafa at this suggestion. 'And, anyway, he can't be drowned,' he said. 'I'd have seen his body.'

'Well, I don't know about that. Bodies don't surface for a few days, and then again, if he's caught in the weeds, he might stay under till he's eaten by the fishes.'

Conchi squealed with disgust and Aunt Meri scolded,

'Don't talk about such horrible things when we're eating.'

Uncle Fat winked at Rafa but Rafa didn't feel cheerful enough to smile back.

For more than an hour Uncle Fat's car toured the lanes and roads and nearby villages. Uncle Fat drove slowly so that Rafa could take in the fields on either side, and the inside of the car was like an oven, even with all the windows open. There wasn't a soul about. Every sensible person was either eating or sleeping at this time of day. Even the dogs and chickens and donkeys were asleep.

When eventually they headed for home Rafa was grateful that Uncle Fat didn't try to cheer him up about Moro or, worse still, say once again, as Aunt Meri had, that Moro was only a dog and that there were more dogs than chocolate. All he said, without elaboration but with feeling, was, 'I had a dog once, when I was a boy.'

Then he started asking Rafa about Madrid, and his friends there, and how Papa could like being a waiter, for ever dishing up meals to people who were too mean to tip like gentlemen. Madrid seemed like another world just then to Rafa. He had lived there all his life and yet all that was real to him just now was this vast and empty countryside, and the one little black dog he was looking for.

When they got back Aunt Meri said consolingly, 'Well, it doesn't matter really, does it? You won't be here that much longer. You just think about your new little sister, and how happy you're all going to be with her. And now go and lie down for a while, and don't wake Conchi.'

Rafa went to the little house where he and Moro had first met. Moro wasn't there. He hadn't been back for ages, Rafa decided. The last bit of straw he'd pulled out of the mattress was sticking up in exactly the same way.

After that he didn't know where to look, and for a time he didn't know what to do with himself. The poulterer saw him in the street and called out, 'Don't you want any chicken legs for Moro. I've saved some for you,' and Rafa dully shook his head.

He kept expecting to see Moro outside the house, dark eyes glistening, tail wagging, and nothing was the same because he wasn't there.

He cheered up when Mama phoned to tell them about the baby. She had jet black hair and blue eyes and her face was still a bit screwed up. She weighed three kilos seven hundred grammes, and she was as good as gold because she didn't cry one bit at night, and hardly during the day either.

Conchi got very excited about all this baby talk. She'd lost some interest in her dolls since Moro had come onto the scene, but now she was busy bathing them again. Aunt Meri showed her how to put nappies on them and she bought her a dummy for the biggest doll. It was too big, so Conchi went round sucking it instead. The more people laughed at her, the more she sucked it. But she hadn't forgotten Moro completely.

'Tell me the story about Moro again,' she demanded of Rafa one night. 'About him being a prince. Is he really a prince, like you said? And when is he coming back?'

'Of course he's a prince and he's not coming back for a while because he's gone to visit the castle up on the hill. They're having a meeting up there.'

'Who are?'

'All the dogs in the world – the ones that have been bewitched, the same as Moro.'

Rafa's ideas began to expand. He remembered those little fat dogs in Madrid. They were there. One was a sultan. Moro and the dogs were talking about making war on people like Pepe. They were going to get their own back.

It was a nice idea, Rafa thought, grinning bitterly to himself in the darkness as he described to Conchi how they would all come pouring into the village one day to chase Pepe's gang into the river.

75

'And will they all drown?'

Rafa thought for a while, but at last said, 'No . . . Moro's not as bad as Pepe. He'll only want to scare him, I expect. Afterwards, he'll let him go, as long as Pepe promises to leave him alone in future.'

'Why don't we go up to the castle and see if he's there?' demanded Conchi.

'It's too far. You'd get tired. Besides,' he added, suddenly feeling full of hurt again, 'it's only a story, and I'm going to sleep.'

The football games weren't the same any more, not half so much fun without Moro, though they did quarrel less and get on with things more. None of the boys wanted to go to the river. They didn't say anything, but nobody suggested it. They roamed around, looking for mischief.

They went bird-catching in the fields, with nets or stones; they chased a few cats, and teased donkeys and mules when their owners weren't looking, until people started shouting at them, 'Why don't you go off to the river? Devils!'

A week went by and Moro was forgotten. No one mentioned him any more, but Rafa still had a sadness for him in his heart.

Then, one evening, just as in a fairy story, Moro was there again.

Rafa was sitting at the entrance to the house, legs sprawled out, looking through the album of football stars he was collecting. You bought the pictures in little envelopes and you didn't know what you'd bought until you opened them. You got lots of repeats and half the fun of collecting was the swapping afterwards, and sticking them in the album. He'd done five swaps that afternoon and was counting up how many empty spaces he had left.

It was growing dark and he just happened to look up when he saw a little dog limping up the street. For half a second Rafa held his breath. Could it be . . .? No. Don't be

76

13

Moro wasn't himself for quite a while. Rafa didn't know what was wrong with him. He didn't know anything about dogs, anyway, but he noticed that Moro's nose was dry and hot, instead of wet and cold; he noticed that he wanted to sleep a lot and spent most of his waking time with his muzzle on his paws. He wasn't interested in anything, he didn't want to play at all, and he wasn't much fun.

'He might have eaten some poison,' suggested Uncle Fat.

'Can't we take him to the doctor?' Conchi suggested hopefully, but Uncle Fat just laughed at this and chucked her under the chin.

Rafa stayed close to Moro while he was like this, much as he wanted to run off with the other boys. He was scared of leaving Moro on his own, defenceless, knowing that Pepe was muttering threats about him, so he sat beside him while he slept. When he stroked him Moro licked his fingers.

Moro didn't want to eat, though he drank plenty of water. Aunt Meri gave him milk, but he didn't want it. Some days his whole body burned. At other times he was restless, getting up, wandering about without knowing why, before curling up again, nose tucked under his tail.

Rafa knew that inside Moro a battle of some sort was going on. All he could do was sit beside him, wait and hope. People would say, 'How's Moro today?' Rafa didn't know if they really cared, or if they just asked because they knew he cared.

Conchi didn't like Moro while he was sick. She wrinkled up her nose because he smelled, because his eye looked horrible.

'Why doesn't he go away again?' she said to Rafa, forgetting he was supposed to be a prince.

Bit by bit, day by day, Moro won his battle. His eyes looked brighter, even the left one which was still lopsided from the cut, and he began nuzzling and pushing at Rafa instead of just sleeping beside him. He began to fight with Rafa's hands, growling and snarling, grabbing hold of his fingers with his strong, white teeth, but with such gentleness that Rafa marvelled. He knew how those teeth could splinter hard bones.

If Rafa had a fight with Conchi, she would really hurt him – pull his hair, bite and scratch him, even when it was supposed to be fun – but not Moro. He wasn't so careful with Rafa's clothes, though, and when Aunt Meri saw any tears in his shirt or shorts he was hard put to explain them away.

Soon Moro was as bouncy and cheeky as ever. All the boys cheered when he darted back into a football game without any invitation. And Moro responded to the noise they made like the clown he was, attacking the ball with such ferocious zest that no one could get it away from him. He played the match almost by himself, while everyone watched and laughed and cheered him on, and when he was quite exhausted, he stood in the middle of the pitch, tongue lolling, tail wagging, obviously feeling very pleased with himself.

But he wouldn't go back to the river again. When he saw Rafa with his towel he stayed sat by the door, and the expression on his face would make Rafa feel quite guilty. Moro's ears would droop flat, the light would die out of his eyes, and he seemed to shrink in size.

'Don't look at me like that,' Rafa found himself saying one

evening, because he knew how much Moro didn't want him to go, but Moro went on looking the same – crushed, defeated, unable to understand. Rafa found himself feeling angry, wishing Moro would leave him alone.

People began to say, 'That dog's going to miss you when you go back to Madrid!'

And Pepe said to Moro one day, in Rafa's hearing, 'You'll see, Moro. You'll see.'

Moro cheekily barked back at him because he didn't know anything about Rafa going away. Pepe just grinned. He could wait.

Rafa didn't listen to what people said because he'd decided that when Papa came to fetch them, he'd take Moro back to Madrid with him. He knew Mama didn't like dogs, but somehow he'd persuade her to change her mind. He knew Papa would understand, because of that little white dog, Perla, he could still remember.

He could make a little house for Moro on the kitchen balcony if Mama wouldn't let Moro in the flat, and after school Moro could play down in the street with him and his friends. Rafa knew Antonio would like Moro, and Moro wouldn't mind about contamination because dogs didn't bother their heads about such things. Rafa didn't notice it either. It was only Papa.

But he didn't say anything to his aunt and uncle because he didn't want to hear them say it couldn't be done. He didn't want them to talk to his parents about it before he did. Grown-ups had a way of spoiling things. He didn't tell Papa about Moro whenever he telephoned, thinking it would be better to surprise him on the day itself – the day for going home.

So Rafa and Moro played the days away, neither of them worrying because Rafa had the future all sorted out, and for Moro the future didn't exist.

One day Rafa and Moro went up to the castle together.

Rafa didn't tell Conchi where he was going because she'd want to come, and spoil things because he knew she wouldn't be able to walk that far. He didn't tell the other boys, either, because he had all kinds of ideas about that castle, which he didn't want to share with anyone.

It was a long way, further than Rafa had estimated. Even Moro began to get a bit fed up with the wearisome trek across hard, stony fields. Twice he got thorns stuck in his pads and Rafa had to pull them out, though Moro managed to pull the burrs off his legs with his teeth. A couple of times Moro sat down, looking at Rafa with head cocked on one side and an expression which seemed to ask, 'Do you know what you're doing? Do you know where you're going? Are you sure?'

'Come on,' Rafa had to urge him.

From a distance, it wasn't much of a hill, but, close to, it was high and steep. Big stones from the castle walls lay scattered here and there. Perhaps they'd been lying like that for hundreds of years. They looked part of the scenery. There were little paths made by sheep, and a few pale blue flowers growing in the shadow of thorn bushes.

Rafa was wearing his uncle's hat again, but when at last he reached the castle he took it off. A bit of a breeze was blowing and it felt good on his bare head.

Uncle Fat had told him the truth. There wasn't much to see. A few tumbledown walls, a Moorish archway against an open sky. Only the view was worth coming here for.

Rafa turned slowly to take it all in – all the land below him, almost completely flat, brown and stony. He couldn't see the river but he knew it was there, amid the trees which looked like a wood from here. He saw the whole shape of the village, a kind of hexagonal, trailing off towards the fields, the church towering above red roofs, white walls and courtyards.

It was like being on his balcony back in Madrid, high

above the street, almost in the sky, and Rafa stared and thought until Moro grew impatient and began barking for attention. Until Moro barked, it was absolutely silent. The breeze wasn't strong enough to create a sound of its own.

'Shut up,' said Rafa. He wanted to be part of that silence a little while longer.

He thought about Don Quixote, wandering across that bare landscape seeking challenge and adventure. It was harsh, painful. No wonder his heat-addled mind turned windmills into giants! Yet it was beautiful. Something within him responded.

Then he looked at Moro, barking again even more impatiently. He swiped his arm at him with a grin and cried, 'Come on. Let's go home.'

They ran down the hill, almost falling over each other, Moro yapping most of the way.

When they got back Aunt Meri's house was full of people, women mostly, neighbours. Uncle Fat was there, too. It was time to eat but there was no food on the table and the cloth hadn't been laid.

Even as Rafa's eyes took these things in – Conchi sitting on Aunt Meri's lap, bewildered and silent; Aunt Meri's eyes all swollen with crying – his mind began to wrestle with the atmosphere he'd suddenly plunged into. But before he could sort it out, Aunt Meri was on her feet, handing Conchi over to one of the neighbours.

'Rafa!' she cried. 'Where've you been? We've been looking for you everywhere.'

'I went to the castle . . .' he began, but he knew she wasn't angry.

She suddenly crushed him into her arms, almost smothering him against her ample breast, and began weeping over him. Rafa just stood there, frozen, hearing the sounds inside her, as if she was breaking up.

He knew before he heard the words. Yet when he heard

83

the words they didn't make sense. All that was in his mind was the view from the top of the hill, which didn't fit in with what Aunt Meri was saying.

'Your Papa phoned. Your Mama . . . In the night. They had to take her to hospital. They did everything they could, Rafa. All the best doctors . . .'

From the top of that hill you could see that the world was round. How could anyone have ever thought it was flat, when it looked so curved from the castle walls? He'd seen photographs like that, pictures taken from aeroplanes, but he'd never seen it in real life before.

Aunt Meri handed Rafa to Uncle Fat. She needed to blow her nose. Uncle Fat put an arm round Rafa's shoulders. It was strange to see him without a smile on his face, without that glint of laughter in his blue eyes. He was a lot older than Papa. Rafa suddenly noticed that his whiskers were grey.

He said something but Rafa didn't hear him. Somehow the harshness, the vastness of that landscape still in his head got inside his heart as well, swelling and swelling till Rafa couldn't breathe or think or see or hear.

He pulled away from his uncle and ran out to the street, where people hung about, staring at the house. Everyone had heard. Everyone knew.

Moro didn't know. When he saw Rafa he jumped up with surprise, tail wagging. Rafa pushed him aside, hardly feeling Moro's legs against his own. He ran down the street, not knowing where he was going, and Moro loped along beside him, jumping up, not knowing that Rafa was gasping inside, crushed by the weight of earth and sky, grey whiskers and a phone call.

Rafa stopped dead. There were some boys on a bare patch between the houses, kicking a ball about. Shouting. Laughing. Moro dashed forward, yapping, always ready for a game. The ball bounced as it always did. The boys and

84

Moro chased it, and Rafa stood there frozen, trying to understand.

How could they be playing football when Mama was dead?

14

Nobody explained anything to Rafa, at least not so that he could understand. They told him about the heart attack, the dash through the streets in an emergency ambulance, the vain efforts of a whole team of doctors. But they couldn't explain to him why one day Mama could be talking to him on the phone with joy in her voice – telling him about the baby, the baptism, reminding him to be good – and then be dead a few days later.

They told him she was in heaven. A special mass was said in church for her, but Rafa couldn't imagine Mama in heaven. He could only think of her at home, cooking at the stove in their tiny kitchen; making a big sandwich for him when he came home from school, while he waited impatiently, thinking of his friends in the street; sitting Conchi on the table to comb her hair and fix it with rubber bands; lots of little things.

Mama was always doing things. Even when she sat and watched television, she'd have some darning, or a bagful of beans on her lap to cut up for supper. That was the only way Rafa could imagine Mama.

He couldn't understand how life just went on as usual. Going to bed, getting up, eating; Aunt Meri washing and ironing, feeding the hens; Uncle Fat working on his house; the sun still shining; Conchi playing with the girls across the street; the neighbours chatting, the shopkeepers selling things. If everything was the same Mama just couldn't be dead.

Sometimes he forgot. He joined in a football game or went to the river; he bought soccer stickers and swapped the repeats with his friends; he laughed and shouted with them. It was always when he went home that everything came back, so he stayed in the streets or in the fields with his friends for as long as he could. He was noisier and livelier than any of them, thinking up jokes, making fun of everything he could think of.

Once an old woman, eyes sharp with contempt, called out to him, 'Aren't you ashamed of yourself, boy? Playing games with your friends when your mother's just died!'

All the boys fell silent with embarrassment. Rafa muttered, 'Silly old woman,' almost before she was out of hearing, but she had broken up their game and very soon each one had a reason for running off.

Rafa and Moro went to the little house in the field. Moro hardly ever went there now and he ran through the doorway with eagerness, as if he'd suddenly remembered the place. He found a grey bone under the bed and trotted about with it in his mouth, while snuffling here and there with excitement. Rafa just stood and watched him.

Moro put the bone down. He looked up at Rafa, tail wagging slowly, and waited, puzzled because he knew Rafa was far away just then. He gave a half yap, half whine, as if to say, 'Come on. I'm here. Do something!' and Rafa responded with a pretend attack, which was his and Moro's favourite private game.

Rafa used his hands, half boxing, half wrestling. Moro used his teeth. Sometimes Moro turned tail and ran, sometimes it was Rafa's turn. Moro attacked Rafa's feet very boldly, pulling at his laces, growling ferociously; and Rafa pretended he was Kung Fu, with lots of grunts and karate chops.

87

Then Moro jumped up on the old mattress, barking into Rafa's face, and Rafa dived on him, trying to pull him into his arms. Moro hated this. He was terrified of being grabbed, even in fun. He cringed and escaped Rafa's hands, then shot off the bed and out of the house.

Rafa started tearing at the mattress, digging his hands into the holes, tossing straw, bugs and dust into the air and over himself. Moro watched from the doorway, aware of the anguish, the anger that went into Rafa's tearing and ripping. He barked excitedly, but he was scared and ready to run away.

Rafa turned to him and Moro retreated, half snarling, struggling against fear but unable to overcome it, bewildered by Rafa's dark mood.

'Go away, then. You needn't hang around me,' Rafa shouted at him. 'I don't care.'

Moro crept away, but only a little distance. When Rafa went back to the village, he followed, further behind than usual and not running here and there. His ears were flat and his tail was still. His jaws hung open, but that was because of the heat, not because of any joy. He didn't know that Rafa wasn't angry with him.

Papa telephoned one night. He said he was coming down in his car in two days' time to take Rafa and Conchi home.

Aunt Meri said, 'They can stay as long as they like. There's no hurry. You need time to sort yourself out.'

But Papa said he was coming.

Aunt Meri said to Rafa, 'Do you want to talk to him?' but Rafa shook his head.

Conchi said, 'Let me, let me!'

She loved talking on the phone. She had a plastic phone at home and she talked into it for ages, pretending she was ringing all her friends. 'It's just as well that's not a real phone,' Papa said once. 'I'd never be able to pay the bills.'

And Conchi had been angry with him because she wanted her phone to be real, and he said it wasn't.

She was excited when she knew they were going home. She didn't really understand about Mama. She'd cried because everybody had cried. She said her prayers, and said a special prayer for Mama in heaven, but she didn't know what that really meant, any more than Rafa did.

Aunt Meri gave Rafa some bones for Moro. A neighbour was in the patio with her just then. As he went out to the street, Rafa heard the neighbour say, 'He's going to miss that dog when he goes back to the capital.' And Aunt Meri exclaimed, 'Woman, if he's just lost his mother, how's he going to miss a dog?'

Papa had said he would arrive in time for lunch, so Aunt Meri cooked a special meal. Rafa didn't want to be there when Papa came. Ever since the phone call he had begun to dread seeing him again. Why couldn't Papa stay away? He was all right here with Aunt Meri and Uncle Fat and Moro. Papa's coming would somehow make it all real, in a way that it still wasn't real to Rafa.

He wanted to be as far away as possible, so he went to the castle again. He sat on the hilltop and looked at the view, feeling the breeze on his arms and face, and Moro lay panting beside him, looking up into his face, though Rafa didn't notice.

He couldn't stay on the hilltop for ever. He had to come down. Everybody had finished eating when he arrived. Conchi was in bed, asleep. Papa and Uncle Fat were still sitting at the table, each with a glass of brandy, and Aunt Meri was doing the washing up. They'd all been talking but the atmosphere was nothing like it had been last time Papa was here. Then there had been laughter, jokes, memories brought to the surface. But Aunt Meri's eyes were swollen, Uncle Fat looked grave, and Papa . . .

89

Papa was like Moro when he had come back sick from wherever he had been, and Rafa hadn't recognized him.

Papa got up and came towards him. He said something. Rafa didn't hear him. He only knew that he was sitting at the table between Papa and Uncle Fat and that the tears just poured and poured down his cheeks, no matter how much he scrubbed his eyes with Aunt Meri's embroidered serviette. And they were saying, 'That's it. Cry. Cry. It'll do you good.'

Only they were wrong. It didn't do him any good. The more he cried, the more and more angry he felt with Papa. Hadn't he promised? Hadn't he said Mama was going to be all right? Hadn't he said he didn't tell lies? And Rafa was crying with anger, not with sorrow.

He was so angry he felt he was breaking in two. He pummelled his eyes with the serviette, soaked and grubby, ignoring the handkerchief Papa was trying to push onto him, and when he couldn't cry any more he went on screwing up the serviette ferociously, unable to bear the hurt that was inside him.

Aunt Meri put him to bed. He slept for a long time, till it was almost time to go to bed again, and then he sat out in the dark street with Moro while they all had supper. He knew they were angry with him because he wouldn't speak to Papa and wouldn't even sit at the table with him. He heard Conchi chattering away happily to him, and his heart ached.

Moro kept pushing him with his nose. He didn't want to sit in the street all night. He'd already slept for hours, waiting for Rafa. But in the end he flopped down again with a sigh and went back to chasing fleas, scratching his ears and chewing his paws.

The next day, at about eleven in the morning, Moro watched with excitement and interest as suitcases and dolls and Rafa's football were put in the little blue car parked in the sun outside the door. There were a lot of people in the street so Moro couldn't get as near as he would have liked.

Uncle Fat put some cans of oil from their own olive trees in the boot, Aunt Meri put in a cheese, wrapped in a cloth, and some eggs from her hens; and a neighbour gave them some cakes and a big jar of fresh honey.

Moro grew more excited and impertinent. Somehow he knew the car was connected with Rafa and he was determined to find out what was going on. Rafa hadn't been out of the house that morning and Moro, expecting him to appear every moment, sniffed and jumped around and ran backwards and forwards, affected by everyone's feelings. At one point he nearly jumped inside the car, but someone frightened him off with a shout.

Rafa came into the street. There were people all round him and Moro couldn't get through their legs. He managed it just as Rafa got into the car, but Rafa didn't seem to see him. He just stared ahead.

'Get out of the way, dog,' someone shouted, almost slamming the door on Moro's head. He ducked and ran round the other side, where Conchi was. The door was still open.

'Look, Rafa,' she cried. 'It's Moro. He's come to say goodbye.'

'Grab hold of that dog, someone,' called Uncle Fat.

Moro dodged as hands grasped for him, running round to Rafa's side again and jumping up at the door. He was getting frantic because Rafa just ignored him. Rafa's father got in the car, slammed the door and switched on the engine as people called and waved goodbye.

'Get hold of that dog,' called Uncle Fat again, with exasperation, making a grab for Moro himself but missing. Several boys started chasing him, Pepe among them. They tried to chase him up the street, away from the car, but Moro kept turning back and dodging them, determined to find out what Rafa was up to, wanting to go with him wherever he went.

The car was moving slowly. Moro came yapping round it, jumping up at the door. Papa pressed the horn to make him get out of the way as he picked up speed. He couldn't go very fast down the lane and Moro just wouldn't leave the car alone. Pepe suddenly got hold of him but Moro struggled like a mad thing, yelping and fighting, springing out of his arms again and loping after the car, followed by most of the boys.

Conchi was looking out of the back window. She saw Moro appear again, galloping through the dust.

'He wants to come with us, Rafa. Look. Look, Rafa,' she demanded, but Rafa just stared ahead, tensing his eyebrows.

The boys stopped chasing Moro, but Moro didn't stop chasing the car. Papa didn't drive as fast as Uncle Fat. His car was too old, for one thing, and he manoeuvred round the holes in the road instead of bouncing through them, so it wasn't too hard for Moro to keep them in sight. But then Papa turned onto the proper road and put his foot on the accelerator. The little car shot ahead.

'Oh,' said Conchi with disappointment. 'He's smaller now. But he's still there. Come on, Moro. Stop, Papa. Stop! Moro wants to come, too. Rafa, tell Papa to stop.'

But Rafa just bit his lips harder and dug his nails into his arms and pretended he was deaf.

Papa said, 'Stupid dog. I almost ran him over.'

Then Conchi called out, 'He's gone.'

She watched the road a little while longer, and then she sat down and talked to one of her dolls because there was nothing left to see.

15

Home wasn't home any more without Mama in it. It was just a place with furniture and cooking pots. There was an emptiness within the walls too vast to be contained. It spread out to the staircase, to the street, even to the market place.

The market place was always full of noise and bustle; women gossiping, toddlers crying, stall-holders shouting about their fish or their melons or their meat. Rafa always went there with Mama on a Saturday, to carry the bags for her. They always went to the same stalls and Mama chatted with the people she knew and argued about prices.

Now the market place seemed empty without Mama's voice.

You couldn't look over the balcony any more to see if she was down in the street, gossiping with a neighbour; and you could never hear her coming up the stairs again, which echoed with every person's footsteps. Mama always came slowly up the stairs, stopping after every two flights. Rafa remembered how she always said, as he ran ahead with the bags and paused to wait for her, 'Oh, I do wish we had a lift in this house.'

It was stranger at home than when they went to stay with Aunt Meri, because everything was different. Everything revolved round Amparito. Even though the upstairs neighbour, Sonia's mother, looked after her while Papa was at work, Amparito was the central figure in everything. Her needs, her comforts, had to be considered before everything else and she was an absolute tyrant, always wanting or needing something, even in the middle of the night.

Rafa had forgotten about the baby till he saw her for the first time, and even then he couldn't feel that she had anything to do with him – that she was his sister, like Conchi. She had tiny, clenched fists and jet black hair and, when she slept, she looked like a frog.

Life became a series of orders and errands. 'Rafa, go and buy a tin of baby food. Rafa, we need some more talcum powder. Rafa, go and see if Sonia's mother has got some clean nappies.'

All Papa did was give him orders. He did the shopping, he looked after Conchi, he put her to bed at night, and when his friends called and asked if he was coming down he had to say no, because Papa was at work and didn't want him in the street.

Conchi was miserable and bad-tempered and wouldn't do anything she was told. Once or twice Rafa slapped her, she was so annoying, and Papa was angry with him when she told him. 'Can't you see she doesn't understand?' he shouted, and he sat her on his knees and gave her everything she wanted till he made her smile.

It was strange seeing Papa in the kitchen, cooking the dinner. He was a good cook, but he didn't have time to make all the things Mama used to make. It was even stranger seeing him change the baby's nappies and feed her.

Conchi wanted to do these things (once she'd got over her original disgust), but Papa said Amparito was still too little. He let her help with powder and pins, and if she promised to sit very still he let her hold Amparito for a few minutes. Conchi beamed with pride and chattered non-stop, smothering the baby with kisses. She was happy when Papa came home.

The only place that was the same was the kitchen balcony where Rafa always sat to think or be alone. Even though Mama hung bits of washing there sometimes, nothing of her was imprinted there. It was the only place where Rafa could forget how everything was changed, and he would sit there for long stretches, screened from the sun by the old green blind and the plant pots wired to the rails.

He remembered how he had planned to make a little house for Moro on this balcony. There was just room for him. He could put some plastic round the rails to keep out the wind and rain, and fix up a shelf over his head. And someone in the market could give him a box to make a bed – not that Moro knew what a bed was. And there were some old dishes in the cupboard to put his food on.

Moro wasn't a big dog, so there was plenty of room, and when Papa was out Rafa could let him run round the flat if he couldn't go down to the street.

Rafa sat and picked all the leaves and flowers off the geraniums, which were dying anyway because no one had remembered to water them, not knowing how else to relieve the pain in his heart.

His anger was still there, that hard, hard anger that had stopped him asking Papa if they could take Moro home; that had stopped him even telling Papa just how much he wanted Moro to go home with them; that even now kept him from talking to Papa, except when he had to.

Papa didn't seem to notice how angry Rafa was, and this made him angrier still. He noticed if Conchi was upset about something. He noticed if Rafa had forgotten to do something. But he didn't once say, 'Rafa, why are you angry with me? Tell me,' or something like that, which was what he longed for every day.

He hadn't thought what he would say to Papa. He hadn't thought he could tell Papa, anyway, without waiting for him to ask. He just let the pain of it gnaw away inside him because, behind his anger against Papa, there was another feeling.

It was really a kind of anger against himself, a kind of guilt.

Mama was dead. In the whole world, nothing worse could happen than that. And yet, when he sat on the balcony to be alone, he kept thinking about Moro instead of about her.

Already it was hard even to remember what Mama looked like. He couldn't exactly see her in his mind. He could remember her doing things, he could remember the things she said, the way she said them. But the way she looked . . .

It was easier to imagine Moro sitting on this balcony with him, squashed against his legs, perhaps licking his knees like he sometimes did in the village. It was easier to remember the way Moro looked at him. Moro's look wasn't just in his eyes, but in his whole body. Mostly it was a look of joy but, sometimes, from his nose to his tail it would be a reproach.

But every time Rafa found himself thinking about Moro he would remember what he had overheard Aunt Meri say to the neighbour. 'How's he going to miss a dog when he's just lost his mother?' It was the tone of her voice he remembered, more than the words. The very idea was unthinkable, the tone said. No one could grieve for a dog when he had his mother to grieve for.

And yet he did grieve for Moro, and wonder where he was right now, and what had happened to him when Conchi lost him from sight on the road. Had he gone back to the village, with Pepe and his gang waiting for him? Had he kept following the car, long after it was out of sight, and perhaps come to a new village and stayed there? Had he been run over, running down the middle of the road like that, and knowing nothing about traffic?

It would be easier not to think about him, if only he knew just where Moro was now, or what had happened to him.

96

But how could he say anything to Papa, without letting him know how much he cared? He could imagine Papa saying what Aunt Meri had said, and he couldn't bear it if Papa said that to him.

So his anger stayed against Papa because he so much wanted to talk to him and yet didn't know how.

One night, about ten days after they'd come home, Rafa had a dream. It was a very bad dream. They were at the river. Mama was there, and Conchi, and the boys from the village, and somebody suddenly said, 'Where's Moro?'

They all looked, and Moro was out in the middle of the river, only now the river had become the big lake in the park, and there were people with rowing boats; and Moro was drowning, but nobody cared. The people in the boats could see him and Rafa was shouting out to them, 'Save him, save him,' but they just went on rowing without even looking at Moro, even though he was splashing round and round in frantic circles.

Mama got up and said, 'I'll save him.' Then, somehow, it was Mama who was drowning instead of Moro, and the people in the boats still went on rowing happily about, ignoring her cries for help. And Rafa stood at the lakeside, feeling how she couldn't breathe, how the water was in her eyes and her nose, her lungs bursting, but he didn't go to save her because he was too scared.

He woke up shouting and sobbing. Papa came and put on the light, so he knew it was a dream. Conchi was still fast asleep in her own bed, surrounded by dolls. He told Papa about his dream, about Mama and Moro, and somehow he expected Papa to put everything right, to make it all a dream – the baby, going to the village, knowing Moro, Mama dying.

But Papa didn't have any special words that could change anything, or make him feel different. Somehow he felt it was Papa who needed words, too; who needed someone to come and put things right for him.

When Papa had gone, and put out the light again, Rafa lay in the dark and felt silent tears slide down each side of his face. And he wanted Moro more than ever, because Moro was the sort of dog that made you feel good, that made you want to shout and run and enjoy yourself.

But Moro was more than a hundred miles away. Or maybe he was dead, too, like Mama.

16

The next day, before going to work, Papa gave Rafa the money for the textbooks he and Conchi needed for the new school year. It was a lot of money because they needed some fifteen books between them.

Papa said, 'And you can buy Conchi a pencil-case, and a new one for yourself, too. Get yourself a good one, but don't spend too much on Conchi's. I expect she'll lose all the pencils after a few days.'

Neither of them said anything about the dream. Perhaps Papa had forgotten it, but it was still very real in Rafa's mind, and he hardly heard Papa reminding him to peel some potatoes and cut up the greens before he came home from work.

Antonio went with Rafa to the shop. He did most of the talking because Rafa couldn't shake off how the dream had made him feel, but on the way back, carrying the books between them, Rafa at last told Antonio about Moro. It was the first time he'd talked about the little dog since he'd come home, and suddenly he poured out the whole story of Moro from the very first day until the last.

'I could have made a really good home for him on the balcony,' he finished, 'but . . .'

To Antonio the silence that Rafa trailed into sounded like despair.

'If I were you,' he said, 'I'd go and get him. Once you've got him, how's your father going to say you can't keep him?'

Rafa halted in the street, startled. Antonio's words conjured up all sorts of possibilities. His heart beat fast at the very thought of having Moro at home. Then it sank again as reality took over.

'It's too far,' he said. 'It's not a ten-minute walk, you know. It's more than a hundred miles.'

Hope thus dismissed, he started walking again, but Antonio persisted, 'It's not like going to the moon, is it? Even that's not far these days.'

He sounded scornful of Rafa's quick surrender. Once Antonio got an idea in his head, he kept at it like a hungry bug. He always believed that nothing was impossible.

'Go and get him, man,' he insisted. 'If you really want him, that is . . .'

The unspoken challenge grated on Rafa but he warded him off with, 'I could ask my father, I suppose.'

'And if he says no? No, man. If you really want him, there's only one way.'

Antonio began to enthuse about all the things they could do with Moro. How they'd be the only gang in the street with a dog that could play football, how they could go ratting with him through the old flats that were falling down; the fun it would be just having him around. And Rafa's heart ached anew as Antonio spoke. Antonio was only making pictures in his mind, but Rafa knew just how real all those things could be.

He crossed two streets in silence, his mind racing with ideas, but not as fast as his heart, which raced with longing.

'I could go on the coach,' he admitted at last.

'That's it!' exclaimed Antonio, slapping him on the back. 'Let's go to the bus station and buy you a ticket. I bet you've got enough money on you.'

'My father will be angry.'

'So what? Hasn't he ever been angry before?'

'Yes, but . . .

'Come on!'

Antonio's eyes gleamed. He was always coming up with ideas and plans, which were often carried out because of his very enthusiasm, not because they were good. Papa sometimes said Antonio was a bad influence. 'One day he'll get all you boys into real trouble,' he warned. But he didn't know how Antonio made everything sound so right and so easy.

'And if your father won't let you keep him at home,' he raced on, 'well, we can keep him somewhere else. There's lots of room in those old houses. He'll live like a lord. We'll all bring him food. We'll all look after him. It'll be great. Don't you worry. Once it's done . . .' and he let the sentence tail away, sure of its effect.

They went to the bus station. A coach was leaving in two and a half hours, just before Papa came home from work, and Rafa had more than enough change from the book money to buy a ticket. Antonio pulled the money from his hands.

'I'll buy the ticket for you,' he said and rushed off to the booking office.

Rafa didn't try to stop him. Papa would be so mad . . . But he'd understand. And Conchi would help. She liked Moro, too. She'd forgotten about him a bit, because of the baby, but Rafa knew he could talk her into siding with him.

He peeled the potatoes and cut up the greens and he told Conchi she had to stay with Sonia till Papa came home. She was happy enough with her pencil case and the new books, and she didn't even ask where he was going when she saw him start off down the stairs.

Rafa was excited now, happy even, just thinking that soon he'd be with Moro again, that Moro was really going to be his dog. He had some bread and cheese in a piece of paper, to last him out till he got to Aunt Meri's, and he had some money to buy a drink on the way.

101

The good feeling lasted in spite of the trouble he had at the coach station, when people started asking him where he was going and why he was travelling alone. The driver didn't want to let him get on the coach, when he saw Rafa had no luggage, but people in the queue got impatient and shouted at him to leave the boy alone. He had a ticket like everyone else, and that was enough.

It wasn't until the coach reached Ciudad Real that Rafa suddenly remembered how Uncle Fat had been waiting for them with the car, that in fact his journey wasn't over, and that he had no idea how to go from here.

Those last few minutes of the journey seemed never ending. Every red light, every traffic jam, every lurching halt or start intensified Rafa's anxiety. He'd spent most of his money on the way, having bought an ice cream and a bar of chocolate as well as a drink. What was he going to do?

Waves of panic made him feel hot and cold in turn, and yet he had to sit there and pretend everything was all right. His legs felt weak when at last the coach had made its final stop and everyone started to get off. The driver must have seen something of Rafa's worry in his face.

'What now?' he suddenly said to him, sarcasm in his voice.

'My uncle's coming to look for me,' Rafa managed to reply, though his voice was forced. 'He's waiting for me outside.'

The driver shrugged. His expression said he didn't believe Rafa, but he didn't want to get involved.

Rafa made for the exit, feeling dizzy and sick. A line of telephone booths made his heart lurch with relief. Of course! He felt in his pockets, and the joy of finding a single suitable coin was almost too much for him.

He had never used a pay phone before but there were instructions on how to do it. Thank goodness he remembered his aunt's telephone number.

His hand trembled as he dialled. All the good feeling had gone. He was tired. He knew he had done something very wrong, and Antonio wasn't there to egg him on or cheer him up. And if Moro wasn't there ... If it had all been for nothing?

Such a wave of misery swept over him that he couldn't even speak when at last he heard his aunt's voice shouting down the phone, 'Hello! Hello! Who is it? What do you want?'

He could hear how her impatience at the continuing silence grew with every word, and his lips trembled as at last he managed to force out, 'Aunt Meri.'

'Who is it?' Again. Crossly. Then surprise. 'Hey, is that you, Rafa? Hey? How are you?'

A pause, but Rafa couldn't speak. His throat was choked.

'But, what's the matter? It is you, Rafa, isn't it?' she shouted.

'Yes, Aunt.'

'And what do you want?'

'I'm here.'

'Here! Where? Can't you talk straight, boy?'

'In Ciudad Real.'

A loud exclamation. Delight? Surprise? Puzzlement crept in as she asked, 'But where's your father? Is he with you? What are you doing there?'

'I'm at the bus station, Aunt. Alone.'

An even louder exclamation. Then, 'Don't move from there. Your uncle will come and fetch you.'

Rafa knew from the way she spoke that she understood, that she knew – not everything, but enough. She went on a bit, shouting down the phone like she always did, but Rafa hardly heard, he was just so glad to hear her voice and feel that now everything would be all right. His lips tasted salty. Then the pips blotted out further words and the phone went dead.

103

On the way to the village Uncle Fat kept saying, 'It's not right, Rafa. It's not right. People don't do that sort of thing.'

He had heard all Rafa's explanations and his face had grown more and more serious. Rafa hadn't known that Uncle Fat could look so grim. All he had said about Moro was, 'Maybe your aunt's right. That dog causes more trouble than he's worth.'

He wouldn't say any more and just then Rafa was too scared to ask. Uncle Fat looked anything but friendly and cheerful.

Aunt Meri first of all enfolded Rafa in a crushing hug, then she scolded. She went on and on, while making him some supper, but Rafa didn't mind very much because it was so good to be sitting there, safe.

Uncle Fat telephoned Papa at the hotel. Rafa was glad his uncle broke the news. He was really scared about talking to Papa. It was no good saying it was Antonio's fault. Really, it was his own.

By the time Uncle Fat handed the telephone over to Rafa, Papa was already used to the idea. Everything was such a surprise to him that he hardly had time to feel angry. But there was hurt in his voice.

'Your uncle says you've gone to look for the dog. Why didn't you tell me you wanted him so much?'

'You didn't ask me,' said Rafa.

Even as he spoke Rafa knew he wasn't only thinking about Moro. He was thinking of all the things he had wanted Papa to ask and to tell him, all the things Papa didn't want to talk about and which hung between them unsaid because both of them hurt too much to talk.

'You're right,' Papa agreed. 'I didn't ask you anything.'

The silence that followed wasn't a bad silence and Rafa suddenly felt all right. He couldn't think of the right words to say – there were both too many and not enough – and eventually Uncle Fat took the receiver away from him and exclaimed into it, 'I don't know what you just said but Rafa here is grinning like a monkey.'

He laughed in that hearty way of his and, when Papa had finished saying something, went on, 'Don't worry. I'll bring him back myself. Tomorrow. Meri will come, too. We can see the baby.'

Everything was all right, everything except one thing. Rafa still didn't know anything about Moro. He hadn't been there, outside the house. Had he really expected him to be? Yes, he had.

'And Moro?' he asked them both, hardly able to breathe for fear of what they might say.

'I don't want to hear anything about dogs,' said Aunt Meri. 'And it's time you went to bed.'

Uncle Fat said, 'Tomorrow.'

'But why can't you tell me now? Just if he's all right, if he came back.'

'Not a thing. You deserve a good hiding, but . . . Go on with you. Get to bed.'

Rafa thought he wouldn't be able to sleep. In fact he slept so long that Aunt Meri had to come and wake him up next morning because it was late and Uncle Fat wanted to be off to Madrid before the day was half spent. Aunt Meri was wearing a smart dress as well as her bracelets and rings, and Uncle Fat was shaved and looking not a bit like a village man, except that his face was so brown.

'And Moro?' Rafa asked again, while Aunt Meri made him drink all the coffee and eat all the cake she'd put on his plate.

He was getting scared. They were going to rush him back to Madrid and then tell him on the way that Moro had disappeared. And he wouldn't get a chance to find out for himself if it was true.

He went out into the street, longing to see Moro waiting there for him, kidding himself that this was the answer.

105

Moro would be there – a surprise. But Moro wasn't there and Uncle Fat was already sitting at the steering wheel, tapping impatiently with his fingers.

'And Moro?' cried Rafa.

Aunt Meri pushed him into the front seat beside his uncle. 'Get along with you. Don't waste any more time. That blessed dog. It's all you think about!'

They set off. Uncle Fat said, 'I've just got to stop by at the new house for a minute, before we get on the road.'

Rafa was too churned up to speak. He couldn't really believe he had come all this way for nothing.

At the new house Uncle Fat got out of the car.

'You coming?' he said to Rafa. 'To take a last look? Next time you come to see us we might be living here. And you can say you helped build it, right? I just want to make sure old Ana's all right,' he explained as they went through to the yard, Rafa following in too much misery to answer.

Ana began to bray. It was the most horrible, stupid noise any animal could make. Suddenly a dog began a high-pitched, slightly hysterical accompaniment.

It was Moro. Rafa knew that bark as well as he knew the sound of his own voice. Then he saw him, straining at the end of a rope, jumping in the air and falling over backwards in his excitement.

Rafa ran to him with open arms, shouting his name, and Moro did another couple of somersaults at the end of the rope before slamming against Rafa's chest and slobbering all over his face.

With his arms still round the struggling dog, hardly able to contain him, Rafa turned to his uncle who was watching with a smile. 'Uncle!' he began, not knowing what to say.

'Blasted dog,' said Uncle Fat. 'I'll be glad to see the back of him.'

'But why's he here? Can I untie him? Can I take him home with me? Say yes, Uncle Fat. Please.'

'I don't want him. I just didn't fancy that Pepe having him, that's all. He's a nasty bit of work, that boy. Moro's worth two of him.'

Rafa turned back to Moro to hug him again and again, and Moro wriggled and squirmed like he always did, scratching Rafa's arms in his excitement, making little whimpering noises between barks, as if he wasn't quite sure what was right for the occasion.

'You'd better have him,' Uncle Fat said. 'He just lies here all day long looking miserable. He's more of a pain than old Ana. He wasn't meant to be tied up. He's a gypsy, is that one. He'd rather be free for a day than locked up for a year.'

'Will he be happy with me?' Rafa asked, thinking of the balcony which suddenly seemed very little after all.

'How should I know? Perhaps he will. Or perhaps he'll run off one day.'

'My friends and I will play with him. We're always in the street after school. We wouldn't tie him up.'

'Then I expect he'll be fine. Come on, let's go. It's a long drive to Madrid.'

Uncle Fat had to cut through the rope round Moro's neck because they couldn't untie the knot, mostly because Moro wouldn't keep still.

He was dusty. There was a fat tick on his ear, as well as the fleas that roamed about quite openly over his belly, but these things didn't worry Rafa any more than they did Moro. This was his usual state, after all. Whether it would do for a city dog was another question, one that neither of them anticipated.

For Rafa at that moment it was enough to have Moro licking his nose, chasing round in circles, jumping in the air and yelping, full of clowning adoration; and a car waiting to take both of them back home.

For Moro . . . Well, he was alive, and Rafa was there, and tomorrow didn't exist.

107